26/1/1980

This copy of

SAVE THE PONIES!
by Josephine Pullein-Thompson

belongs to

_____

_____

Josephine Pullein-Thompson

Save
the Ponies!

SPARROW
BOOKS

A Sparrow Book
Published by Arrow Books Limited
17–21 Conway Street, London w1p 6jd

An imprint of the Hutchinson Publishing Group

London Melbourne Sydney Auckland
Johannesburg and agencies throughout the world

First published 1983
© Josephine Pullein-Thompson 1983

Set in Linotron Baskerville
by Rowland Phototypesetting Ltd
Bury St Edmunds, Suffolk

Made and printed in Great Britain
by Anchor Brendon Ltd, Tiptree, Essex

isbn 0 09 932360 5

To Elizabeth Paterson, who shared my travels and Alexandre and Nadia Blokh, but for whom we would never have known 'The Island'.

Contents

I

I knew it would be awful

'It's no use you keeping on at me, Mandy. With a foot full of sea urchin spikes there's no way *I* can drive you to town,' said Mrs Brake, who, large and fair and plump, lay stretched comfortably on a sunbed, dark glasses lending an air of determination to her expression. 'If Dad won't take you you'll have to walk.'

'You know Dad won't. You heard him just now. He's in a bad mood: the car's got something wrong with it and he's trying to mend the loo cistern, only he keeps making it worse.' Mandy Brake was large and brown-eyed like her mother, but she had mouse-coloured hair, cut in a fringe and tied back in a pony tail.

'I'm sure we *could* walk there; that must be it,' said Kate Morrison pointing at the hill, covered in small, white houses, which rose from the sea, southwards along the coast. 'We might meet some of the little horses, or at least a donkey, if we walk.'

'It's too hot,' wailed Mandy, 'and we've got to bring back all this shopping,' she added, looking at the list her mother had given her.

'The shops shut at lunch-time,' said Mrs Brake in a warning voice. 'The guide book says that everyone in this place takes a siesta and nothing opens up again until about seven.'

'It's a dump,' complained Jeremy Brake angrily. He was standing on the low wall which divided the terrace from the steep hillside, covered in shrubby plants and thorny bushes, through which a little path zigzagged down to the cove. 'I wanted a swimming pool and a diving board, I told Dad so, but he wouldn't listen. You wouldn't have trodden on a sea urchin if we'd had a pool.' Jeremy was large and brown-eyed like his sister, but his hair was darker, almost black, and cut short so that it fitted his head, a thick, cropped skull cap. Fergus Stapleton, who stood on the wall beside him, was small and thin with straight fair hair. He was shading his blue eyes with a hand as he gazed out to sea.

'It's not a dump; I think it's terrific,' he told Jeremy. 'I've never seen such a dark-blue sea. And look at those mountains,' he pointed to the great, blue humps which filled the sky beyond the town, 'I can't wait to get up there.'

'If the car's a dud we're not going to get anywhere,' snapped Jeremy. 'We're just stuck in this boring place for the next ten days; I hate holidays.'

Kate sat on the wall feeling miserable. It wasn't just home-sickness, she had always known that a holiday with the Brakes would be a distaster and already she was being proved right. Her mind went back to the wet, cold day in March when Mrs Brake had insisted on driving her home from school, and then surprised them all with the invitation. The house had been a mess with nappies everywhere, Thomas was yelling, he'd just started teething, Lucy was being difficult because – having been the baby of the family for eight years – she resented Tom grabbing her position and Emma who, at ten, held firm opinions and despised tact, was making her worse.

'We want to take Kate on holiday with us,' Mrs Brake had shouted above the racket. 'We're renting an

enchanting little cottage on a Greek island for a fort-night at the beginning of August. Georgeous sunshine, no pollution, our own bathing beach; Mandy wants to take Kate, she say's she's her best friend. Roy, Man-dy's Dad, says it's all expenses paid. She'll just need pocket money, he'll see to everything else. We're tak-ing Fergus Stapleton to keep Jeremy company. It seems absurd, we had our two close together so they'd be companions for each other, but it hasn't worked. They just don't get on. Last year they ruined our holiday in Spain, they fought night and day. Roy said that he'd never do it again, either we'd take a friend for each of them or we wouldn't go.'

Mandy had never been *her* best friend, thought Kate. Sue Preston and Carol Miller were her friends at school, but Fergus, who went to a different school but also helped at the riding stables, was a friend. The fact that he was coming had been one of the small consolations as she fought a losing battle with her mother. Fergus, and the breed of little horses which Mrs Kark, the owner of the riding school, said lived on the Island.

'You can't miss a chance like this,' Mrs Morrison had said, beginning to load the washing machine as soon as Mrs Brake had gone. 'With four of you we're never going to be able to afford Greek holidays; it's a wonderful opportunity, Kate, don't be a fool, of course you must go.'

'They're too rich,' Kate had complained. 'Mandy has everything. She's always got the latest in clothes and records, she had a television for her last birthday and she has loads of pocket money.'

'That's life,' said Mrs Morrison, 'there's always someone richer than you and someone poorer around. Even if you started everyone equal they wouldn't stay that way; you have to get used to having friends who are richer and poorer than you are.'

'It's so difficult,' Kate had tried to explain, 'Mandy's always buying ice creams and if you say you haven't any money she tries to lend it to you and, if you won't have that, she buys you the ice cream. She doesn't understand that some people can't have everything.'

'It's tiresome,' Mrs Morrison had agreed, 'but you can't let minor problems stop you from doing really exciting things.'

Her father had agreed with her mother. Brushing aside her protests that she had planned to help at the riding school and ride in the Twelve and Under Gymkhana, he said, 'You'll be a very dull person if you never go abroad,' and rushed out to buy her a Greek phrase book.

Her mother, taking her shopping for new summer clothes, had said, 'I want you to have a good time. Being the eldest you've always had had to take a lot of responsibility, especially since Tom arrived; it'll be good for you to get right away from us all and really enjoy yourself.'

But I'm not enjoying myself, thought Kate dismally as she sat on the white-washed wall of the terrace and stared out to sea, I wish I was back at home, even with Tom yelling and Lucy grizzling. Mandy and Jeremy behave like big editions of Tom and Lu, but you can't just tell *them* to shut up.

Fergus, who was good at shutting out the difficulties of life and enjoying the present, stopped gazing at the mountains and looked down at Kate. She was small for her age with thick auburn hair, which grew in a smooth, shining chunk. Her eyes were grey and her face, with its small nose and mouth, usually wore a rather anxious expression, but now it looked positively despairing. He'd better do something, he decided, and stepping down from the wall he interrupted the Brakes who were both moaning at their mother. 'Look, there's a huge sandy beach along there, it must be on the way to the town, so when we get too hot we can have a swim and then walk on again. Do you think we can take the rucksack hanging on the back of the kitchen door? It'll hold most of the shopping.'

'Yes, let's go,' agreed Kate quickly, 'I'm longing to explore.'

'I'll have one last go at Dad,' said Mandy making for the shower room.

'Here, these are for the shopping and these for your lunches,' Mrs Brake was counting out drachma notes and giving them to Jeremy. 'Don't forget the olive oil, the guide book says it's the best thing for sea urchin spikes, it loosens them.'

Kate, who had been given endless warnings about sunburn by her mother, hastily pulled jeans and a shirt over her swimsuit. The boys had done the same, but when Mandy came rushing down from the bedroom she shared with Kate, she was wearing very short pink shorts, a yellow T-shirt and high-heeled sandals. Jeremy looked at her and groaned rudely. Fergus, shouldering the empty rucksack, said, 'Right, we're off,' and led the way up the steep zig-zag path to the road.

Their own cove was wild and rocky and two neighbouring white, cube cottages also looked down on waves beating and battering against a stark and rocky cliff, but beyond the cottages and their crooked, scrubfilled gardens, where the road bent and then ran closer to the sea, the beach began and there was a path leading down to it.

The sun was burning hot and there was no shade. As they trudged along the road Kate began to look forward to a swim. Mandy kept stopping to take stones out of her sandals. At first the others waited patiently, but Jeremy became more and more irritated and when she stopped for the third time, he shouted, 'Oh come *on*, Mandy.'

'I can't, I've got stones in my sandals,' his sister shouted back.

'Well why did you come in those silly shoes, you stupid twit,' shouted Jeremy in a rude voice. 'Why didn't you wear track shoes like everyone else?'

'How was I to know that there'd be all these little stones,' Mandy screamed back.

Fergus and Kate looked at each other. 'It's a lovely place,' said Fergus smiling his crooked smile. He sniffed the air, 'It doesn't smell a bit like England.'

'No, hot and herby,' agreed Kate, 'and it doesn't sound like England with the cicadas making all that racket.'

'When you can hear them above the Brake racket, which sounds *very* English,' observed Fergus as he took the path to the beach. 'You can take them off here, Mandy,' he shouted back, 'it's sandy.'

Mandy, who was lagging further and further behind, finally reached the beach and took off her sandals, but then there were fresh wails, 'The sand's absolutely baking, it's burning my feet.'

'Good, I hope it burns them off,' Jeremy shouted back. 'I can't stand this,' he added in an exasperated voice, 'tomorrow we're going on our own, Fergus, and the girls can teeter about in silly shoes on their own.'

'Kate's OK, and Mandy'll learn,' said Fergus calmly. 'Walk in the sea,' he shouted back at her.

Kate decided to paddle. She took off her shoes and

wandered miserably through the small, pouncing waves. It was going to be horrible if Fergus and Jeremy went off together, Mandy would never want to do anything interesting, she just liked being driven about by her parents. Fergus is the only one I like, Kate thought gloomily. I *hate* all the Brakes. It's going to be a really horrible holiday; why did Dad and Mummy make me come? I *told* them it would be awful.

'Kate, hoof marks,' shouted Fergus from the beach.

'I expect it's only donkeys,' Kate answered despondently as she waded back to the shore. 'I counted five of them on the quayside when we arrived.'

'Too big for donkeys, look.'

'Mules then,' said Kate.

'Could be, but where there are mules there must be horses, or ponies,' Fergus reminded her. 'These look quite fresh. I think there are two of them and they're definitely going the same way as us,' he decided on closer inspection. They began to hurry forward, walking faster and faster until they were jogging. They had forgotten the Brakes. Jeremy followed slowly, demanding, 'What's so exciting about a few hoof-prints?' but getting no answer, while Mandy, finding herself ignored, had begun to run along the edge of the sea in an attempt to catch up.

Then furious at the neglect, Jeremy began to demand a swim. 'Stop,' he called. 'I'm hot, let's have a swim now. It's no use going on, you can see the beach gets more and more crowded the nearer you get to the town.'

But at that moment there was a triumphant shout from Kate who had caught sight of the ponies. There were two of them, picking their way carefully through the sunbathers, the sandcastle-building children and the groups of young men playing with bats and balls: a black and a grey roan, ridden by a boy and a girl. Capless, they wore only shorts, T-shirts and sandals. Without a word Kate and Fergus ran in pursuit, and as they came alongside, found that the riders rode bareback. The boy looked Greek, tall and slim with black, curly hair and black eyes. He sat loosely on his pitch-black stallion, who , though only about thirteen hands, looked taller for he carried himself proudly. The girl was slim, with brown, curly hair and dark eyes in a tanned face, she looked very at home on her little pink mare.

'They've only got headcollars,' observed Fergus slowing to a walk.

Kate took a deep breath, '*Kaliméra*,' she said with her best Greek accent. And then, realizing that she couldn't possibly manage a sentence, she reverted to English. 'What lovely ponies.'

The girl smiled at her, 'Thank you. Mine is young, only four years old. She is called Mya. Nico's is called Vrondi – Thunder.'

'Hullo,' Nico looked down on Kate, his face, sun-burned to a deep golden tan, was unsmiling.

'Hullo,' she answered. 'I'm Kate, this is Fergus Stapleton, those two coming along are friends of ours, Jeremy and Mandy.'

'You are English and you stay here?' asked the girl.

'Yes, we're on holiday, staying at a cottage, about a mile along there,' Fergus explained. 'We only arrived yesterday.'

Kate was patting the ponies. 'We all ride in England, but at a riding school; we don't have our own ponies. Is Mya yours?'

'She is really owned by my grandfather, but he has

given her to me; he has other ponies. Vrondi belongs to a farmer called Mr Pappas, but as Nico works for him in the holidays and after school, he is allowed to ride Vrondi.'

'And you live here?' asked Fergus.

'I live here all the summer and Athens in the winter, Nico lives here all the time.'

'No saddles and bridles?' asked Jeremy inspecting the leather headcollars and rope reins critically.

'No, no one bothers with them on the island. My grandfather has a bridle, I thought of using it tomorrow for the race, but all the other riders will have headcollars.'

'Race?' repeated Mandy.

'Yes, it is the annual race tomorrow. I am riding in it for the first time, we have been training every day for two weeks, galloping on the beach. Mya is not fast and she is in foal, so I must not ride her too hard, but Vrondi has a good chance; he and Nico came second last year.'

'Oh we must go to it, Daddy's got to get that silly car going,' decided Mandy. 'Are you Greek?'

'Half. My name is Sophia Perdika, my father is Greek, my mother English.'

Vrondi was getting restless; Nico spoke to Sophia in Greek.

'We must go. Perhaps we will see you at the race tomorrow.'

'Yes, but where is it?' asked Fergus.

'In a field outside the town. You follow the signs marked "Camping" and they are building the hippodrome in the field beyond the camp site. It will start at nine-thirty, they say,' Sophia called over her shoulder as Mya chased Vrondi along the beach.

'Oh dear, I wanted to ask if they were the ancient

17

breed of little horses and if there was a riding school on the island,' said Kate gazing after the disappearing ponies.

'They didn't look like horses to me, more like Welsh ponies,' Jeremy sounded contemptuous.

'You can ask her tomorrow at the race,' Mandy pointed out. 'We've definitely got to go; I'm going to bully the life out of Dad if he hasn't got that stupid car going.'

'Even if there isn't a riding school, there must be a farmer who hires out ponies,' decided Kate.

'Who wants to ride ponies of that size, and bareback?' asked Jeremy scornfully.

'I do,' said Kate suddenly feeling bold. 'I'm not going to spend any of my money until I find out.'

'It'll be pony rides on the beach,' scoffed Jeremy.

'There's no sign of that at the moment,' said Fergus. 'It would be marvellous if we *could* hire ponies and ride up into the mountains; I'd love to explore up there,' he added looking longingly at the huge, blue humps.

'It would be great if we didn't have to walk everywhere,' admitted Mandy.

They swam. The sea was warm but cooling. Unfortunately the cooled feeling didn't last long, when, finding that time had sneaked away and it was already half-past twelve, they had to hurry up the steps from the beach and go in search of the town.

The shops were in the old town and a narrow way led up through white, cube cottages, separated by rough, steep triangles of land on which goats were tethered, kids bleated and skipped, chickens scratched and empty stables smelled of absent donkeys. As they climbed higher, the white cottages clustered closer. The streets were too narrow for cars and led off to even narrower alleys, with stone steps climbing up between the houses. Mandy lagged and moaned, stopping at intervals to smear suntan cream on her scarlet arms and knees, but when, close to the top, they found the shops, she was miraculously restored and vanished with a whoop of joy into one that sold souvenirs. Jeremy made a dash to the forecourt of another where flippers, snorkling masks and beach balls were displayed among a bright confusion of plastic buckets and bowls, water carriers and hoses.

Kate sighed. 'I suppose we'd better do the shopping.'

'Yes, come on, you can try out your Greek again. That looks the right sort of shop.'

'They ought to help,' grumbled Kate who was feeling hot and cross.

'It'll be easier with only two of us,' observed Fergus. 'I'll go and get the shopping money off Jeremy before he spends it on some touristy object.'

'Tell him not to spend the lunch money,' said Kate. 'I'm desperately hungry.'

The shop was small and dimly lit but you could choose what you wanted from the crammed shelves and the owner was agreeable.

'You English or German?' he asked, adding up their bill on a sheet of paper, there was no cash till.

They found another shop with fruit and vegetables and then, laden with the rucksack and two plastic bags, they went in search of the Brakes.

'We've got everything but the bread,' Fergus announced proudly.

'I asked where you bought bread, but I couldn't understand the answer,' Kate explained. 'It seems to be down that way.'

'Look what I've bought,' shrieked Mandy. She was wearing a red, peaked baseball cap and waving some new sandals, a T-shirt and a china donkey.

Jeremy showed them two bats and a ball and a clasp knife ornamented with a picture of an ancient galley, with figures straining at their oars.

'I thought we could play games like those guys on the beach,' he told Fergus.

'Where are we going to have lunch?' demanded Mandy. 'How much cash did Mum give you, Jeremy?'

'We must find the bread shop first,' said Kate gazing down the street.

The walk home during the hottest part of the day, when all sensible people were taking a siesta, felt like an endurance test. Mandy moaned that her new sandals were giving her blisters, but Kate and Fergus, burdened with the shopping, refused to pay any attention, and even Jeremy was too hot to quarrel. It was in an exhausted silence that they slithered down the zig-zag path to the cottage and collapsed round the big table under the vine.

'Oh you are a treasure,' said Mrs Brake hugging Fergus who, trying to check the purchases against the list, looked highly embarrassed. 'Mandy and Jeremy never bring home more than half and Roy's not much better.'

'Kate did just as much as I did, and her Greek's better than mine,' said Fergus refusing to take all the credit.

Mandy grabbed a bottle of mineral water, 'Only three, they're not going to last long,' she complained. 'You ought to have bought at least a bottle each *and* some coke.'

'Who would have carried it home?' asked Kate, 'you wouldn't help with what we had bought.'

'It's insane renting a cottage with water you can't drink,' grumbled Jeremy. 'Don't be such a pig, Mandy, there's no need to drink the whole lot.' He grabbed the bottle from her. 'Ugh, it's warm, and there's no fridge. Dad must have been out of his mind actually choosing a dump like this with no electricity.'

'Where is Dad?' asked Mandy. 'There's a pony race tomorrow at nine-thirty and we know two of the riders, we met them on the beach, so Dad's simply got to take us. Has he got that stupid car going?'

'He's gone into town to change it and to buy a washer for the cistern and a spray to kill beetles; apparently there's a whole colony of huge red ones under the calor gas cooker.'

'What a dump,' muttered Jeremy.

2

The race

Mr Brake, who was plump and red-faced with thick, brown hair, a moustache and brown protruding eyes, liked the idea of the pony race and spent the evening preparing his cameras. The difficulty of reading, or playing any of Jeremy's card games, by oil lamp, especially as Mr Brake would only allow the tiniest of flames in case they blackened or cracked the glass shades, drove everyone to bed early, with the result that they all wakened much earlier than usual, and were on the terrace eating melon for breakfast, and admiring the sun climbing higher and higher over the sea, by seven-thirty. By nine they were all waiting round the replacement car, which Jeremy said disdainfully was even more of a banger than the first, while Mr Brake assisted the still-limping Mrs Brake into the front seat.

There were no signposts pointing the way to the town. With only one tarred road on the island, winding its way across the centre joining the tiny port on one side to the town on the other, the inhabitants obviously though signs unnecessary. But where, close to town, the road divided, a notice announced 'Camping' and an arrow pointed along the lower road above the sea.

'Left, Dad, left,' shrieked Mandy.

Jeremy was grumbling about the car, 'It's burning oil, Dad. Can't you smell it?'

'The brakes work and the clutch works,' his father

answered, 'and that's more than you could say for the first one. The chappie at the garage told me that all the cars here are completely clapped out, it's the roads, or the tracks they use as roads. . . .'

Kate dug her elbow into Fergus. 'Ponies,' she said softly.

'Race horses,' said Fergus with a grin. They gazed out at the two long-legged boys riding a grey and a bay.

'They're not as good-looking as Nico,' announced Mandy.

'If you ask me the whole thing's going to be pretty grotty,' complained Jeremy. 'They're all going to be bareback and in headcollars and those two haven't plaited their manes or anything.'

'I think it's rather nice; you obviously don't have to be rich to ride,' argued Kate. 'Though I agree the ponies could do with a groom.'

'Right, Dad,' shrieked Mandy. 'There it is, beyond the camping field. Look, there are masses of people going in.'

They joined a jam of cars. The drivers were excitable, hooting their horns and revving up their engines as a crowd of brightly dressed holiday-makers threaded their way through and a mule, long-eared and serious looking, with four straw bales piled high on his wooden packsaddle, squeezed past from the opposite direction.

'I'm certainly going to get some pictures today,' said Mr Brake in satisfied tones. 'No sunbathers on the beach this year, but a real slice of Greek life. Pity about your foot Cynny, or you could have driven while I shot this lot.'

'Dad's dotty, he enjoys looking at his snaps and showing off his films when he gets home much more than the actual holiday,' Mandy explained to Kate.

'There's Sophia,' said Kate as the car advanced into

a sudden space, 'and that must be the hippodrome.'

'It doesn't look much like an English racecourse,' Mandy sounded disappointed.

The field, by far the largest and flattest they had seen on the island, was of golden stubble. The corn had been recently cut and bales of straw lay about everywhere. Some had been arranged as seats around the course which was square and had been fenced off by stout posts, with rails along their tops, and more rails, criss-crossed between the posts, filling in the gap below. There was an outer and an inner fence and it looked as though the ponies would race round the track between the two, which had been harrowed to make the rock-hard ground soft and dusty.

'No green turf, no white paint, no grandstands, disgraceful!' announced Fergus in a pompous voice. 'Don't you agree Jeremy?'

'I do. These foreigners have no idea,' said Kate stifling a giggle. 'Whoever heard of a square race-course?'

'Do stop Dad; can't you park here? I want to go and talk to Sophia and I don't want a ten-mile walk,' wailed Mandy.

'You can't park here, it's in full sun. We'll be roasted alive when we come back. Can't you find some shade?' demanded Jeremy.

'Right, all kids out then. I'm going to drive your mother over to the rails.'

They began to run back, dodging through the crowd, to where they had seen Sophia. But there was soon a wail from Mandy. 'Wait for me Kate. This stubble's prickly, it's making holes in my feet.'

Kate sighed and waited. 'Why must you always dress up so?' she asked. 'It's much more comfortable in jeans and trainers.'

'She won't learn, she's too thick,' Jeremy, walking on, shouted back over his shoulder.

'She doesn't understand that this island is country, real country, with goats and sheep and proper fields, not a suburb like Ralston,' said Fergus waiting for Kate.

'I'm not dressed up; everyone wears dresses and sandals at the seaside,' argued Mandy hobbling after them.

Jeremy had found Sophia but couldn't think of anything to say.

'How's Mya?' asked Kate patting the pink neck.

'She is a little nervous, but I am much worse; I am nervous for myself and for Nico,' Sophia answered with a forced smile.

'I've counted twenty-three ponies so far,' announced Jeremy, 'but they look a pretty ropey bunch; nothing as good as Vrondi.'

Kate looked round, most of the ponies were hitched to the sagging barbed wire which fenced the field: bays, browns, blacks, duns and greys, they stood patiently, with hanging heads and half-closed eyes, dozing in the still, gentle, morning sunshine. Two, who were awake, were giving angry squeals every time they touched noses, others were having their photographs taken by the mainland Greek families who seemed to make up most of the crowd. Doting fathers were plonking little children on the ponies' backs and snapping them with expensive cameras.

'You can't call those two ropey.' Kate pointed across the field. Two grey stallions were surrounded by a group of boys who seemed to be inciting them to fight. One stallion was almost white. High-crested and proud in carriage, he was obviously in the prime of life. The other, iron grey and less powerful in build, looked younger. As they reared up and boxed with their fore hoofs the boys cheered. The ponies squealed and bit, then reared again.

'It's a good thing they're not shod,' said Fergus hearing the blows thudding home.

'That's Mr Pappas, Vrondi's owner,' said Sophia as a small, swarthy man wearing what seemed to be the farmers' uniform of trousers, short-sleeved shirt and straw hat, hurried towards the boys, shouting at them in Greek. 'He also owns Hyóni, the white stallion, who breeds excellent mules. Hyóni is very popular with the farmers, but Mr Anesti, the president of the Island Horse Society will not register him in the first grade of ponies because he is too large and has imported blood.'

'He looks lovely, rather like the bigger sort of Welsh pony,' observed Kate.

'Surely it's time they got started,' said Jeremy with an impatient glance at his watch.

'What staggers me is that there don't seem to be any girl riders,' Fergus told Sophia. 'In England it's the other way round; at least, there's usually about five girls to every boy.'

'The Island girls do not ride, it is not considered correct; they are very quiet and old-fashioned. In Athens plenty of girls ride, but there it is very expensive. As I am half English, I do not count as an Islander so I can do as I please. My grandfather does not mind me riding, but he does not like the idea of the race. He will only let me ride Mya, who has no chance. He has found boys to ride his faster ponies, Libertas and Kima.'

'How mean can you get? Now I've heard that I'm really glad I don't live here,' decided Mandy.

'It might be fun changing things,' suggested Kate.

'I'd start a special race for girls and some showjumping classes.'

'I like this,' said Fergus who was examining the spoon-shaped piece of leather, decorated with a turquoise ornament, which dangled in the centre of Mya's forehead.

'It's a charm,' explained Sophia. 'You need them today because all the horrible characters like Andony Komas will be going round trying to put the evil eye on other people's ponies.'

'You don't believe that, do you?' Jeremy sounded scornful.

'It happens. They come up and praise your pony, that's the most usual way, and he suddenly goes lame or starts colic. I think I'd better go and put my name down. Will you hold Mya for me?' she looked at Kate. 'Don't let anyone admire her. Well, it doesn't matter about the tourists, but not the Islanders and especially not Andony.'

'Which is he?' asked Kate looking round anxiously.

'The fat one, over there. Fat and quite fair, wearing a red T-shirt and cantering about on a dapple grey.'

Mr Brake appeared, a camera swinging from either shoulder.

'You've got hold of a pony already, that's a bit of luck. Up you get Mandy and I'll take a picture.'

'No, we can't ride her, she's just about to go in the race,' Kate told him hastily. 'We're looking after her.'

'Well stand in a bit closer then. Jeremy, get behind Kate, that's better. Now Fergus, you sit down in front of the pony. Great. All look this way, smile.'

Sophia came running back. 'We are going to have the parade now,' she told them. 'We lead the ponies round the track for everyone to see. You must go and find a place by the rails.'

27

'I'd hate to be the only girl,' said Mandy as they hurried towards the rails. 'The boys aren't paying poor Sophia any attention at all; even Nico's pretending she's not there.'

'Oh it's not that bad. I've been the only male in the ride at Mrs Kark's,' Fergus told her.

'That's quite different, you weren't cold-shouldered, made to feel you oughtn't to have been there.'

They found Mrs Brake sitting on a bale of straw and looking bored.

'The sun's beginning to get hot,' she said, 'I wish I had a parasol. Do put on some more tanning lotion, Mandy, your nose is catching the sun and the last thing I want is a permanently red-nosed daughter.'

'No, that would be the last straw,' agreed Jeremy. 'Mandy the red-nosed reindeer,' he chanted.

'Oh shut up,' Mandy hit out at him.

'Here are the ponies,' said Kate hastily. The riders were now wearing large home-made numbers on their backs, most of them were boys of fourteen or fifteen and they looked very tall walking beside their ponies, none of whom was more than thirteen hands.

But there was one boy, a smaller edition of Nico only his skin was even darker and his black curls tighter, who didn't look more than ten and was obviously frightened of his pony, a very pretty, slender youngster, brown with a white blaze.

'They'd all get nought for turnout at the most hope-less pony club rally,' announced Jeremy scornfully as he looked along the line of riders who were mostly dressed in jeans, T-shirts and trainers. A few wore shorts and sandals, one had bare feet. The ponies too had a workaday look; only the charms on their head-collars showed it was a special occasion.

'Yes, and what would Mrs Kark say? Bare feet and

not a crash cap in sight,' added Mandy for once in agreement with her brother.

'Well, I suppose it's not *so* dangerous as the ponies aren't shod,' said Kate, 'I mean kicks on the head and having your toes stamped on are nothing like so bad with a plain hoof.'

'Who's going to win, that's the question?' said Fergus looking at the ponies carefully. 'Vrondi seems fit and eager to go, which is more than you can say for some of them. That bay, number nine, looks fast, and the taller of the two iron greys.'

'I quite like the look of Andony, whatever Sophia says. At least he's cheerful and talking to everyone,' Mandy pointed out. 'He's not being silent and stuck up like Nico.'

'Nico's probably got the needle,' Kate defended him. 'Now what's happening, they're all going out?'

'They're getting into heats, you didn't think they'd race the whole lot at once, did you?' asked Jeremy.

There seemed to be a lot of argument about who should be in which heat and while the boys protested and the officials shouted commandingly, most of the ponies went back to sleep. One enjoyed a very thorough roll in the dust of the harrowed track, only a few, Vrondi among them, seemed at all excited.

'Nico's in the first one,' announced Fergus as the argument ended and six ponies came forward and lined up, their riders standing beside them.

Suddenly, at the starter's command, the riders vaulted on and the ponies surged forward. A tall boy, his long legs wrapped round the belly of his bay pony, took the lead. Vrondi, who had started slowly, and an iron grey disputed second place. Behind them the pretty, brown youngster bucked. It was a huge buck. His rider shot into the air and landed on his back with a painful-sounding thud. To Kate's surprise he jumped up smiling and pursued his pony round the course. The others raced on. Nico and Vrondi had drawn ahead of the iron grey, but the long-legged boy on the bay seemed to have an unassailable lead. Then, as they came into the fourth corner, the bay stopped abruptly. Ears back and eyes rolling he began to nap towards the entrance. The iron grey, going fast and not very steerable in a headcollar, ignored his rider's frantic tugs and cannoned into the bay. The riderless brown vanished through the exit, a stout, dun mare tried to follow him, but was shooed back on course by the crowd. Nico, taking the shortest route on the inner rail, avoided the mêlée and swept on. Followed by a tiny, very white grey, he started the second circuit. The English cheered him loudly as he raced past, but the long-legged boy had got his bay going again and was gaining on Vrondi length by length.

'The bay's the faster,' said Jeremy in an excited voice, 'he's going to catch Nico.'

'Come on Nico, come on!' they shouted at him frantically, as he came round the top end and put on a spurt for the winning line. At the same moment the bay swerved towards the exit again. This time his rider was ready for him and whacked him with the rope reins, but Nico, with a quick look back, raced on and won by five or six lengths. The bay was second, the iron grey a bad third.

'Well done, Nico,' they shouted, and, hearing English, he looked round and waved.

An official appeared with a loudhailer, he made an announcement in Greek and the second heat came in.

'There's Sophia,' said Mandy. Mya's strange pink colour made her easy to pick out. She was against a cream pony, a black with a star and a white snip on his nose, two bays, one very lively and the other half asleep, and another of the little white greys.

'Mya needs waking up,' announced Jeremy. 'Sophia ought to get her on her toes.'

'How do you know? You've never ridden her,' Mandy began, shrill and argumentative.

'I think the lively bay will win,' Fergus shouted her down. 'What do you think Kate?'

'The cream,' Kate picked him at random, 'but I'm going to cheer for Sophia.'

The start was very dramatic. The ponies shot forward swerving and bucking in an entangled mass. In a moment there were three or four riders on the ground, but they were vaulting on as fast as they fell off. Suddenly Sophia emerged from the scrum and set off at a brisk canter. Finding they had a leader, the other ponies decided to join in, four of them with riders. Sophia held her own on the first circuit, but then it became obvious that Mya was tiring. The sleepy bay and the cream pony passed her and fought out a neck and neck finish, no one seemed sure which had won.

The third heat was a fiasco. Except for Andony Komas, the riders seemed much less experienced than in the earlier heats, and a boy with brown, curly hair, who rode a very fast, brown pony, raced round the first circuit with an enormous lead, but then pulled up, thinking he had won. The spectators shouted at him to go on, but he looked at them uncomprehendingly until the other ponies thundered by, then understanding at last, he galloped in pursuit; but it was too late. Andony's little grey, though carrying much more weight than the other ponies, flew round, neck streched out, ears back, and won.

The fourth heat started well, but piled up in a nappy heap when they came to the exit corner.

'They don't use their outside legs. Mrs Kark would soon get after them,' said Fergus.

'Still, it must be difficult, bareback and in headcollars. I bet you wouldn't do any better,' Mandy argued.

'Maybe not, but I'd love to have a go.'

'So would I,' agreed Kate. 'But not on an unknown pony, I'd like Bodkin or Seagull.'

'If only Sophia and Nico had been in this heat, they'd have won easily,' moaned Mandy when, on the second lap, most of the ponies made for the exit again, allowing an iron grey with a large head to win at a leisurely canter.

'You can't say that, their ponies might have napped too,' Jeremy told her.

Mandy made a face at him, 'I can say what I like, and anyway it's true, isn't it, Kate?'

'I'm wondering whether to go and look for Sophia now. I must ask her if there's anywhere you can hire ponies and I might miss her in the crowd at the end.'

'Oh wait till after the final,' Fergus advised. 'Look at the crowd behind us, and they're six deep all along the rails; you won't see a thing if you move now.'

'Now, don't you go wandering off on your own, Kate. We don't want to lose you as well as Roy,' instructed Mrs Brake from her straw bale. 'And what's all this about hiring ponies? You can all ride in Ralston. Surely we've come here for the beach and the sun and the swimming; the things we can't have at home.'

'It would be a different kind of riding,' explained Kate.

'I'd love to ride up into the mountains; you can't do that in Ralston,' Fergus supported her.

'I don't think I want to ride miles and miles bareback in this heat,' objected Mandy.

'Oh why don't they get a move on?' asked Jeremy

in an irritable voice. 'What *are* they arguing about now?'

'Let's try a slow handclap,' suggested Mandy.

'It looks as though extra people are trying to get into the final,' said Fergus standing on the edge of Mrs Brake's bale and gazing up the course. 'Oh I think he's letting in the two who dead-heated.'

They watched the five ponies line up. Nico and then Andony on the inside, the cream pony, the sleepy bay and the iron grey with the large head grouped together on the outside of the course. This time Vrondi was very keyed up. He knew what was coming and pranced and twirled nervously as he waited for the starter's command. It came, and Nico was quickly away. Andony went with him, the dapple grey's head level with Vrondi's black flank. The cream stayed within striking distance, but the iron grey and the bay were soon trailing lengths behind.

'Come on, Nico,' Mandy encouraged him. 'I want to know the winner. I'll get Dad to take a photograph of us talking and drive everyone at school mad with jealousy.'

No one paid her any attention; they were too intent on the race. Nico was still on the inner rails, still held his lead of half a length, with the cream pony two lengths behind Andony. The rider of the sleepy bay had fallen off when his pony swerved towards the exit, but, as the leading three came round for the second time, he remounted and continued, in front, but a lap behind.

The crowd was roaring. Lying low on their ponies' necks, legs driving, the boys raced on. The dapple grey was inching up, she drew level with Vrondi, for a moment they raced neck and neck, then she began to tire, strength and youth told, Vrondi started to draw away. The bay was cantering sedately ahead of them in the middle of the course. Andony shouted at him urgently, and the boy hauled on his rope rein turning the pony towards the inner rails. As they came, galloping flat out for the finishing line, Nico was suddenly trapped – the rails on one side, Andony on the other, the slow pony ahead. He tried to pull out, but Andony urged the dapple grey to even greater efforts, and Vrondi was going too fast to be controllable in a headcollar. He swept on, apparently hoping to force a way through the rapidly closing gap between the bay and the rails. Before he reached it, the gap vanished, the black pony braked, there was a crash and a splintering of wood as he met the rails. Andony crossed the finishing line and, waving one arm above his head in triumph, proclaimed himself the winner.

'Foul, obstruction or whatever it's called in racing,' said Jeremy. 'There ought to be a steward's enquiry.'

'I think Nico's hurt,' Kate watched anxiously as he slid off Vrondi and then leaned against the pony, his face pale and rigid with pain. Various people ducked under the rails and ran to him. Mr Pappas, looking grim below his straw hat, strode down the course to inspect his pony. Andony who had been acknowledging the roars of the crowd, sitting on his pony waving his joined hands above his head, set off on a lap of honour round the course.

A fierce argument began between Mr Pappas and the officials; the boy on the sleepy bay defended himself shrilly.

'It's maddening not being able to understand,' complained Mandy. 'Why doesn't Sophia come and tell us what's happening?'

Nico was still massaging his knee, but his face had returned to its normal colour. He began to protest too, pointing across the course, arguing vehemently, but he didn't seem to make much impression on the flint-faced officials, and Andony was allowed to continue his lap of honour.

'Poor Nico, what a shame,' said Kate turning away. 'Why don't we go and find Sophia?' She looked at Mrs Brake. 'If we do get lost we can go to the car and wait.'

'I wish I could speak Greek, I'd go and join in. Tell them what we saw,' said Fergus fiercely. 'I'd give anything to know what Andony shouted to the boy in front.'

They edged their way out of the crowd and then fought their way into an even thicker one round the course entrance where all the ponies and riders seemed to have gathered. As they reached Sophia, Nico came limping out, leading Vrondi, and the other riders surged round him asking questions.

Kate and Fergus looked at each other and sighed. 'If I ever come here again I must learn some more Greek,' Kate decided.

'We never go to the same country twice, so it's pointless,' Jeremy told them. 'Besides most people speak English.'

'Not when anything exciting happens,' argued Kate.

Mandy had squeezed closer to Sophia and was tweaking her T-shirt. 'What's happened? What's going on, do tell us?' she demanded.

Sophia turned, 'Nothing very good. Andony is to be allowed to have things his way.'

'Oh, he's not. It's not fair. Everyone saw what happened, they ought to at least re-run the race.'

'Here, here,' added Fergus.

'No hope I'm afraid. Andony's father is one of the officials and his uncle's the mayor. If Mr Anesti – the president of the Horse Society – was here he wouldn't have got away with it, but no one else is strong enough to stand up to the Komas family.'

'What *did* Andony shout at the boy on the bay?' asked Fergus.

'To get out of the way, to get on the rails,' answered Sophia.

'Of course Mr Komas says he meant the outer rails, but Nico is sure he didn't. If he had held his tongue they could easily have passed one on either side of Stephan. An then it was at the very moment when it came to him that he was going to lose, that he shouted.'

'There must be *someone* you can appeal to,' Jeremy sounded very indignant. 'A chairman or vice-president or someone.'

'Mr Anesti is president, chairman and secretary all rolled into one,' said Sophia shrugging her shoulders hopelessly.

Kate began to ask about hiring ponies. It didn't seem a very good moment, but she had a feeling that this was one of those days when the right moment never comes.

'There is no riding school or trekking centre on the Island,' Sophia answered, 'but Mr Pappas might hire some of his ponies. How many do you need, one for each of you?'

'I'm not sure about Jeremy yet,' Kate told her, 'but certainly three.'

'I'll find out and let you know. My grandfather might let you have Kima, but he is particular over Libertas. Can you all ride? The Island way – bareback and headcollars?'

'Yes, Fergus and I ride a lot bareback. But how will you let us know? Our cottage has no telephone.'

'Can you come to my house tomorrow morning, not too early? It is next to the Ionis Hotel, there is an iron gate into a garden. If you cannot find it ask for the Perdikas, everyone knows us.'

'Thank you very much,' Kate tried to sound as grateful as she felt. 'About twelve then.'

'Good. I must go now,' Sophia explained, 'something else has happened. That very dark man over there, the one with the smiling face and many gold teeth, is a horse dealer from Athens. It seems he is trying to buy some of the little horses and Nico is very worried, he is afraid that Mr Pappas may agree to sell Vrondi.'

'Did you hear that?' asked Kate, turning to the others as Sophia pushed her way into the group of boys surrounding Nico.

'Yes, it's awful, because Nico really does seem fond of Vrondi,' said Mandy, 'but I suppose Mr Pappas must have other ponies he could ride.'

'You can't exactly prevent a farmer selling his ponies,' agreed Fergus, 'I mean he breeds them to sell and make money; but it's certainly not Nico's day.'

Jeremy, silent and suddenly impatient to get away, led them briskly through the fast-dispersing crowd to the car. Mr and Mrs Brake were already there and had opened all the doors and windows in an attempt to cool it down.

'Well , kids, did you enjoy that? I took some really wonderful pictures,' Mr Brake told them enthusiastically. 'And I met a Greek-Canadian back here on holiday. He told me a perfect place for us to have lunch. A taverna on a sandy beach – not a sea urchin in sight – and right off the usual tourist track. Oh get in,' he added irritably as Jeremy and Mandy began to complain about the scorching state of the car's interior. 'We won't have time for a swim before we eat if you keep messing about.'

3

Riding at last

The lunch at the taverna on the beach and the swimming were a great success; only Mr Brake's complaints about what he called 'the sanitary arrangements' and Jeremy's insistence on endless games of bat and ball cast a slight shadow on the general enjoyment. And, as this expedition was such a success, Mr Brake decided that they would make another next day.

Kate had gone to bed hoping that he would change his mind in the night, but in the morning he seemed equally determined and after several arguments with Jeremy over places, routes and whether the car was likely to survive the journey, he announced that he had picked a beach on the other side of the Island.

Squeezed in the car, between Mandy and Fergus, Kate felt very dismal. She knew it was her own fault; she shouldn't have arranged to see Sophia at twelve, she couldn't expect the Brakes to fit in with her plans, and she just had to hope that Sophia wouldn't be too offended.

The beach was really a series of little beaches round a sheltered bay, and clumps of pine trees growing in the sandy soil made patches of shade.

'What a perfect place,' said Mrs Brake enthusiastically, 'and we've got it all to ourselves.'

'Not bad, not bad,' agreed Mr Brake. 'That must be the taverna up on the hill. I hope it has a few more mod cons than we found yesterday. *Now* what's the matter,' he added as Mandy and Jeremy, who had reached the water's edge, began to shout indignantly.

'It's no good.'

'There are billions of jellyfish – the stinging sort.'

Kate, who'd been walking slowly, ran down the beach with a lightening heart. Shoals of pink jellyfish, ranks and ranks of them, floated in the shallow water, as though waiting for victims.

'Ugh, no one but a maniac would go in there,' said Fergus.

Mandy had run on to the next beach, 'There are billions here too,' she shrieked, 'simply billions.'

'Why do you have to exaggerate so?' asked Jeremy in an irritable voice. 'There are probably a few thousand, a million at the most.'

'Billions,' shouted Mandy defiantly.

Mr Brake insisted on marching along the bay in both directions to see for himself.

'Oh do come on, Dad, I've told you it's no good. Why waste time, let's go somewhere else,' demanded Jeremy.

'Hopeless, quite hopeless,' said Mr Brake, joining the rest of them at the car.

'I told you that ten minutes ago,' snapped Jeremy.

'The Greek-Canadian bloke didn't mention jellyfish, so they can't be there all the time. Well, we'd better go back to the town beach.'

Kate was delighted; she could easily slip away from there and see Sophia. Mrs Brake was longing for a cup of coffee, Mandy for an ice cream and even Jeremy raised no objection, so they drove back quite cheerfully. It wasn't until they were out of the car and running down the steps to the beach that they noticed there were no swimmers.

'Oh *no*, not here too. I don't believe it,' protested

Jeremy. But they were. Rows and rows of them, drifting pink blobs with drooping tentacles.

'This place is useless,' Jeremy shouted at his parents. 'There's nothing to do but swim and now we can't even do that.'

'I'm bored, I want to go shopping,' whined Mandy. 'Can I have some money, Dad?'

'You've had masses of money,' Jeremy turned his anger on his sister, 'look at the rubbish you've bought already.'

'I haven't,' Mandy spat back sounding like an enraged cat, 'and it's nothing to do with you, so shut up.'

'Stop it, Mandy,' commanded Mrs Brake.

'Why should *I* stop, *he* started it; you always pick on me.'

Mr Brake groaned, 'Must we have these histrionics on top of everything else?'

'We could go and see if Sophia's found any ponies for hire,' suggested Kate. 'She said she'd try.'

'Oh yes, great!' Mandy's ill-temper vanished. 'Kate and I can go riding and the boys can go off on their own.'

'Hey, I'd like to ride,' protested Fergus gently. 'You know I want to explore the mountains.'

'Can we have some money for hiring ponies, Dad?' demanded Mandy.

'I've got some of my own,' said Kate. 'I'd rather ride than buy things.'

Mrs Brake looked anxiously at Jeremy, 'What about you, darling?'

'Oh I'll go along and see,' Jeremy decided ungraciously, 'but I'm not going to ride some boring little twelve-hand pony.'

'We're a bit big, but if we'd made the Prince Philip Games team we'd be riding them,' Fergus pointed out.

They found Sophia's house without difficulty. The narrow garden, through which a path led to the house, was dim and cool. Vines, trees and red, exotic flowers met overhead, banishing the glaring heat of the midday sun. Sophia, barefoot and wearing shorts and a T-shirt, came hurrying to meet them.

'My mother is out, she is giving an English lesson,' she explained. 'But I have talked to my grandfather and to Mr Pappas. We can have the ponies: Mr Pappas will hire two, Rozi and Yani. My grandfather will lend two, provided that I go with you. He will not allow the stallion Libertas to go with strangers.'

'That's great, that's terrific!' Mandy was all smiles.

'Yes, thank you *very* much,' added Kate.

'Would you like to try them now, to decide which you will each ride? Just for a short distance as it is hot. Tomorrow we will start early and go far.'

'Oh yes, please,' Kate looked at the others.

'Definitely,' said Fergus.

'May as well,' agreed Jeremy.

'We can't wait,' shrieked Mandy.

Sophia put on some sandals and led the way along a cobbled alley, which took them round the foot of the old town and away from the sea. In a few minutes they reached a dusty road and stubble fields, then Sophia turned in at an open gate and said, 'This is my grandfather's farm.' The stable was low and built of stone, but just the right height for goats and ponies, inside it was dark and cool. Mya and a larger, stronger, iron grey mare stood side by side eating out of the same manger. The stallion was tied in a separate stall.

'Kima and Libertas – Wave and Liberty – you saw them both at the race,' said Sophia.

'Yes that's right. He was the bay that nearly beat Vrondi, wasn't he?' asked Fergus pointing at Libertas.

'That's right, he was really fast,' agreed Jeremy looking at the pony admiringly. 'I wouldn't mind riding *him*, he's taller than most of them.'

'And I'll have Kima,' decided Mandy. 'She's sweet.'

Fergus and Kate looked at each other and sighed.

'OK, but how do we find Mr Pappas's place?' asked Fergus in a resigned voice.

'It is a very short distance. The next farm that way,' Sophia pointed along the road. 'Nico should be there and we will follow in a moment.'

Kate and Fergus walked on through the dust and the heat, past a field of grey-green olive trees with goats tethered beneath.

'The Brakes do rather grab everything, don't they,' said Kate, who was a bit hurt by the way they had allotted themselves ponies.

'I suppose they think if Mum and Dad are paying they ought to have first pick. It'll be a joke if Mr Pappas's ponies turn out even better.'

Mr Pappas's farm had tiny stubble fields and a tiny olive grove. In front of his small white house, a patch of land, caged in wire netting against the goats, was lush with flowers and vegetables: beans and ripening tomatoes stood in neat rows, cucumbers, marrows and huge yellow melons dangled from the netting.

Nico was waiting in the huddle of sheds, all small and crooked, leaning haphazardly, furnished with wooden hayracks and mangers, and smelling of hay, donkeys and goats as well as ponies.

There was no smile of welcome on Nico's face. He looked at Fergus. 'You, Yani,' he said pointing at a stout, dun mare with black points and an eel stripe. 'You, Rozi,' he pointed Kate to a little grey mare, turned white with age.

'No arguments allowed,' said Fergus untying Yani.

'It would have been fun to hear him ordering the Brakes around like that.'

They led the ponies out, tied the headcollar ropes into reins, and vaulted on.

'Ooh, Rozi's got a sharp backbone.'

'Yani feels like a well-stuffed sofa; I'll swop after a bit if you like.'

Nico limped out, leading Vrondi, and then mounted cautiously from a bank.

'How is your knee?' asked Kate speaking slowly and pointing.

'No good,' answered Nico shaking his head. 'Vrondi, OK,' he added pointing to a graze mark on the black pony's shoulder.

Kate and Fergus were used to riding without saddles and bridles. Helping at Mrs Kark's stables entailed a good deal of fetching and taking ponies to distant fields, 'but Mandy and Jeremy, who always had proper lessons in the school or went for hacks, looked far less at home.

'Her back's terribly slippery,' shrieked Mandy riding down the road.

'At least I've got a bridle,' boasted Jeremy who looked equally uncomfortable, 'Sophia says Libertas can be obstinate.'

'I don't think I'm crazy about Kima,' Mandy told Kate. 'I'd swop with you only Rozi's backbone looks even spikier. What's your pony like, Fergus?'

'Sedate and cushiony, but I've only walked a couple of steps.'

Sophia and Nico seemed to be talking busily, but Kate, afraid that they might have heard Mandy's ungrateful criticisms, announced loudly, 'Rozi's lovely and all the others look terrific.'

'We've decided to take you through the water

gardens and perhaps to the chapel on the hill,' Sophia told them. 'It will be much cooler than the coast road or the beach at this time of day.'

'Great,' agreed Kate firmly, for she could see that Fergus was casting longing looks at the mountains and hear Mandy beginning to moan that she was thirsty, and hoped that they were going somewhere where you could buy drinks.

At first the rough road circled the old town and they could look up at the steep, twisting steps; the narrow, cobbled streets and the press of small, white houses which seemed to cling to every inch of the round hill, but then they took a path between stone walls and, riding downhill, found themselves in a different world. A stream about four feet wide splashed and brimmed its way along the floor of the valley. Patches of tall, sweetcorn and carefully cultivated vegetable plots bordered its banks. Huge frogs hopped about and returned to the stream with loud belly flops; a vast orchestra of cicadas vibrated away at their never ending refrain. The path was shaded by the tiny orchards of orange, lemon and pomegranate trees.

Jeremy had ridden alongside Sophia and was asking questions about the different plants and trees. Mandy, not to be outdone, jogged in pursuit of Nico and began to question him, but the Greek boy scowled and made helpless one-handed gestures. He didn't attempt to answer.

'You're not much good at English,' Mandy pestered him. 'You don't want to learn?'

'No, it is not that, usually he is very good,' Sophia spoke for Nico, 'but today he is very anxious, Mr Boukaris, the horse dealer, has made Mr Pappas an offer for Vrondi. Mr Pappas said it was not enough money, but Nico is afraid that the horse dealer will be back with a bigger offer soon; he is buying many of the little horses.'

'Oh *poor* Nico,' Mandy sounded shocked.

'Doesn't Mr Pappas need a pony to work on his farm?' asked Jeremy.

'No, like all the farmers here he prefers mules or donkeys for the ploughing and the carrying of loads. Horses are not so strong and they need more food. Vrondi is a good stallion, but there are many stallions on the Island and Hyóni, as I told you, is the best for breeding mules while others, like Libertas, are registered in the first grade. They have the characteristics of the true Island horse and are used by the breeders who want to keep the breed pure.'

'Why is the horse dealer buying so many ponies?' asked Fergus, 'I mean, is it usual, does he come every year?'

'No,' Sophia shook her head, 'it is a mystery; no one can understand it, except perhaps the Komas family. Andony is working for Mr Boukaris. He is taking the ponies to some central place, but he will not tell where. It seems that mares are being sold as well as stallions, though everyone knows it is against the law to export mares from the Island. If Mr Anesti were here he would put a stop to it, but no one else will dare to stand in the way of the Komas family, they are too powerful.'

Nico suddenly pulled up and, turning to face the others, said, 'I know Vrondi all his life. I train him, I think of him as my best friend. It is not possible that I let him go.' It sounded like a carefully prepared statement and Nico's face, set in hard lines, gave no clue to his feelings, but his voice was harsh and full of pain that would not be disguised.

Fergus spoke first, 'We understand and we are very sorry,' he said.

'Is there anything we can do to help?' asked Kate.

'Have you any money, or could you raise the money to buy him?' suggested Jeremy. Nico shook his head.

'Nico's family is poor, his mother is a widow,' explained Sophia, 'and they have no land so they have no use for a horse.'

'Well perhaps it won't happen; perhaps the old horse dealer won't offer any more,' said Mandy cheerfully, she didn't want the ride spoiled by gloom. 'And even if he does buy Vrondi he may re-sell him to a lovely home; to a family who want a gymkhana pony.'

'I don't think the Greeks have gymkhanas or pony clubs,' argued Kate.

Mandy had lost interest. 'Fergus, can I try Yani?' she asked, 'do you mind swopping for a bit?'

'No,' Fergus slid off the dun and took the grey. 'Yani's nice and round, well upholstered,' he said. 'Want a leg up?'

They rode on in gloomy silence. Nico had taken the path leading up to the chapel and it was hot now that they had left the shade and the stream. Mandy broke the silence. Jogging alongside Kate, she said, 'I like Yani far better than Kima, she's much more comfortable. I'm going to have her tomorrow.'

'What about Fergus, does he want to swop?' asked Kate indignantly.

'He doesn't mind what he rides. Mrs Kark puts him on all the duds, all the obstinate and unschooled ponies, and he never complains. Besides, he's thin and small for his age like you; you're all right on spindly, narrow ponies.'

They reached the chapel and were looking inside the small, whitewashed building, when they heard the patter and scrape of unshod hoofs on the path below. Looking down, they saw Andony Komas riding his dapple grey and leading two other ponies, tied together on a long rope.

Sophia and Nico conferred in urgent whispers. The English children watched Andony, waiting for him to look up and see them , but he seemed intent on his own affairs and passed below them at a brisk jog.

'We are going to follow him, we want very much to know where he is taking the ponies,' Sophia spoke softly. 'Nico knows the ponies he leads and they have been bought by Mr Boukaris.'

'He's not taking them home then?' asked Fergus.

'No, that is the Komas's farm.' Sophia pointed to a white house and buildings on the plain below. 'They have very good land. No, he is taking them towards the cemetery and from that road he will reach the main road and then he can turn towards the port or take a track into the *voonó* – the mountains. Do you wish to come? It will be a problem to take you home, but I have promised my grandfather that I will not let you ride alone.'

'We'll come.'

'Of course we'll come,' Kate, Fergus and Jeremy spoke together.

'Must we?' asked Mandy, 'my legs have begun to ache and I'm dying of thirst.'

'Don't be such a wet,' Jeremy turned on her, 'typical, of you to start wanting drinks when things are getting exciting.'

'Yani belongs to Mr Pappas, so I suppose you could go home on your own, but you don't really want to, do you?' asked Kate.

'No, of course she doesn't,' said Fergus. 'Aching legs and thirst pass off after a time, it's like getting your second wind.'

They climbed the uphill track and passed the dark

green spires of the cypress trees which guarded and sometimes shaded the glimmering white tombs. They lost Andony for a time but when they reached the crest of the hill, they could see him again. He was crossing the main road, taking the path into the pine forest, heading for the great blue humps of the mountains which towered above the climbing trees.

They followed him, keeping the same discreet distance.

'It's a good thing these ponies aren't shod or he'd have heard us long ago,' Fergus remarked to Kate as they crossed the main road. 'I rather miss the clatter of shod hoofs, it's exciting when you go out in a really big ride; you begin to imagine you're part of an invading army, or a victory procession.'

'Yes, it's terrific when we take all the Kark ponies to a gymkhana,' agreed Kate, remembering with a sudden pang that she was missing the Twelve and Under.

The pine forest was dark and comparatively cool. It was a great relief to be out of the fierce heat of the midday sun. Kate was wearing jeans, and she had unrolled her shirt sleeves to protect her arms and turned down the brim of her straw hat to shade her face, but the backs of her hands and her ankles had been burning since they left the shade of the water gardens. She couldn't help worrying about Mandy, whose rather fat arms and thighs had turned a vivid scarlet.

'Don't they hurt?' she asked, pointing at Mandy's legs, 'They look awfully scorched.'

'No, they're just burning a bit, but it's great to be out of the sun. Will you carry my dark glasses for me, my pocket's too small?'

'The ponies are pleased too,' said Kate taking the glasses. She could see that they were all carrying their heads higher, pricking their ears and sniffing the pine-smelling air, as they climbed the winding path of beaten red earth. All round them towered the pines, not growing comfortably on a gentle slope, but perilously from rocks and crags and steeps. And beneath them a glossy green shrub fought for space and red earth.

Sophia pointed at the shrub and said, 'In the springtime there will be many beautiful flowers.'

'Ought we to give the ponies' backs a rest and lead them up here?' asked Kate, rather appalled at the steepness of the hill. Sophia laughed, 'No, they are used to it. Hold the mane in the steep places so that you do not slip back and make it harder for them.'

'You certainly miss stirrups going uphill,' complained Jeremy.

The ponies, clouds of flies buzzing round their heads, climbed on, nimble and uncomplaining, until they reached a plateau where the pines grew thick and dark and the path levelled.

'It feels as though we're on the top of the world,' said Kate.

'Well we're not; you wait till you see what's out there,' snapped Jeremy pointing at the round glare of light which awaited them at the end of the tree tunnel.

'I know, but it still *feels* high,' Kate told him mildly.

'Can I have my dark glasses back?' asked Mandy.

Nico and Sophia reached the edge of the forest first. They looked anxiously down the rocky slope, which plunged steeply to a narrow valley. They looked across the valley to the hill, barren and sandy, which rose on the other side, and then muttered to each other in Greek.

'We haven't got to go right down there and then climb all the way up on the other side, have we?' wailed Mandy.

'Oh I'd love to,' said Fergus gazing at the mountains

49

beyond, each range throwing up peaks to cut the horizon, 'it seems stupid not to explore them now we're so close.'

'We'd need food and water and feeds for the ponies,' objected Kate.

Then there was a shout and they all turned to see Andony cantering along the edge of the forest towards them. He no longer towed the two other ponies; instead he carried a long stick which he was brandishing like a spear. He shouted again and there was no mistaking the aggression in his manner as he wrenched the dapple grey to a halt a few feet from Nico and began a slanging match. Nico shouted back with equal ferocity. Sophia joined in, but she sounded calmer and more reasonable.

The English children looked at each other.

'Do you think that's a weapon he's carrying?' asked Fergus.

'I do, definitely.' Jeremy was looking round. 'And I think we'd better find one for Nico in case it comes to a fight.'

'Oh don't encourage them,' objected Kate, as Jeremy rode Libertas into the trees.

'I think if he realizes he's outnumbered, that he's got to take on all of us, it might cool things,' decided Fergus and, assuming a grim expression, he rode forward and then halted Kima so that she stood squarely beside Vrondi.

'Oh what *is* it all about? I do wish they'd speak in English,' complained Mandy.

'Here, take some of these.' Jeremy came back leading Libertas and carrying an armful of sticks.

'They're none of them long enough,' complained Mandy.

'I know, but they're better than nothing. You take this one Kate and give it to Nico if anything starts; I'll try and find something better,' said Jeremy handing her a stout cudgel and then vaulting on Libertas.

'That one's rotten,' decided Mandy, throwing it into the bushes, 'I'll keep these two for Fergus and me.'

'We can't fight five to one,' objected Kate.

'Yes we can, if he starts it,' argued Mandy.

Jeremy came cantering back brandishing a pole like Andony's. 'Here, I've found a stack of these over there, and he's tied the two ponies to a tree. Do you want it?' He offered the pole to Nico.

'Good, thank you,' Nico answered in English, as he took the pole and balanced it in his hand. Sophia held his other arm and talked to him earnestly in a low voice, but he pushed her away; they could all see that his blood was up, that he wanted to fight.

The two boys faced each other on the red path, it was wider and flatter here at the end of the forest and the sun blazed in through the final archway of trees. Sophia joined the English children.

'He will not listen,' she said despairingly. 'He thinks only of the race and of settling old scores. He will not consider what I tell him; that this cannot help Vrondi; that he will make things worse.'

'But what's Andony so worked up about?' asked Mandy.

'He objects to us following him. He says we are to clear off and stop spying on him. I think we should agree to this, but Nico is so proud and angry he refuses. He wants this battle, but if he wins it will only make Andony more full of hatred and more determined that Boukaris shall have Vrondi.'

The two boys, who had been hurling insults, suddenly rode forward. Carrying their poles as a jousting knight carries his lance, they charged, making vicious jabs at each other's chests. But the ponies swerved away and the poles missed their targets. Kate was glad they didn't have bits and bridles, as she watched the boys haul their ponies round, using all their strength, and kicking wildly, ride at each other again. This time Nico managed to hit Andony with a sideways swipe. Enraged, the fat boy aimed a blow at Nico's head, but, leaning sideways, Nico took it on his arm and slashed back quickly.

'Mind the ponies,' called Kate uselessly in English.

Sophia repeated the cry in Greek, but the boys ignored it. They went on hitting and jabbing, the poles cracking against each other or finding their targets with a softer thud. Nico, taller and the possessor of longer arms, seemed to be getting the best of it; he was landing the most hits and Andony was using his pole defensively, trying to ward off Nico's blows. Then one blow, which Andony parried, cracked down on the grey pony's head, hitting her between the ears, right on her sensitive poll. She stood shaking her head with pain and Kate, remembering an illustration in an old veterinary book, shouted, 'Be careful, you'll give her poll evil. Do make them stop, Sophia.'

But Andony, scarlet with anger, retaliated with a savage blow, smashing his pole against Vrondi's muzzle and shouting out in triumphant revenge as the stallion reared up and swung away.

'That was cruel,' Kate shouted at Andony.

'It's no use yelling at him, he doesn't understand a word,' Fergus told her, as they watched the two boys trying to force their ponies back into the battle. They tugged at their rope reins, kicked and shouted, but the little grey stood obstinate, ears back, shaking with fear. And Vrondi reared, then reared again, higher and higher, determined not to approach Andony.

'Leave it, Nico.'

'Be careful, he'll go over backwards in a minute.'

'Oh come on, can't we go home now, it's getting awfully late,' the English children called to him.

Nico shouted at them angrily. Sophia answered him. He dismounted and threw Vrondi's rope reins at her. Then. shouting insults and brandishing his pole, he advanced on foot. As Andony dismounted and started tying his pony to a tree, another voice rang out and a boy wearing jeans, a T-shirt and carrying a shepherd's crook, appeared at the end of the tree tunnel.

'It is Petro, that is good,' said Sophia. 'You know him, he was in the race and rode Libertas. He looks after his family's sheep on the mountains.

Petro seemed to be asking what was going on, then Andony and Nico both answered him at once, shouting each other down. Petro spoke again, very quietly. They could tell that he was acting as a peacemaker even though they couldn't hear what he said.

Suddenly both boys threw down their poles. Andony untied his pony, vaulted on and cantered away through the trees. Nico, still angry-eyed, came to take Vrondi. Petro followed talking earnestly.

'Sophia, do tell us what he's *saying*,' demanded Mandy.

'He has told Andony that he will see we do not follow him, or watch where he goes, but he tells Nico that he will help us find the horses, he will watch himself. His family do not approve of the mares being sold, but his uncle has sold a stallion to Boukaris, and was told that they are all going to a circus.'

'A circus?' The English children looked at each other.

'But why should a circus want so many?'

'And why have they bought such a mixed lot, none of them match, do they?'

'You'd think Boukaris would have taken a lot more trouble choosing; he'd want very intelligent ponies if they are going to be taught tricks.'

'What does it matter what they're going to *do* , a circus will be quite a nice home,' said Mandy cheerfully. 'We can stop worrying; they're bound to be well treated and given plenty to eat. They'll be better off than they are on the Island.'

No one else felt entirely happy about the circus and, as they rode downhill through the pine forest, they puzzled over ways that the ponies might be used and discussed all the circus acts they had ever seen. Nico led the way, his face set and angry, and, though she cast him anxious glances, Sophia let him ride silent and alone.

When they came out of the forest it was almost unbearably hot and the rest of them fell silent, enduring thirst and heat stoically, as they followed Nico along a shorter and different route, back to the Perdikas' farm. There they let the ponies drink greedily from the trough while Sophia fetched a jug of water and glasses for the riders. They all drank and drank.

'Tomorrow it will be much better,' said Sophia, 'we start early and go by the coast road before it is too hot. You will be here at eight, yes?'

'Yes,' answered Jeremy, while the others groaned at the thought of early rising, but then agreed that it was only sensible.

Kate and Mandy took the Pappas ponies home, saying goodbye and thank you to the still silent Nico, who managed to grunt and wave a hand in reply.

Jeremy suggested going into the town for food, but everyone else cried out in horror at the thought of extra walking. Then Mandy said she had seen a small cafe from the car that morning, and she knew it was on the

54

way home. Jeremy tried to undermine her confidence saying that *he* hadn't seen it and Mandy's places either didn't exist or were closed. Kate and Fergus told him that he was mean and sided with Mandy until she found her cafe. But then *she* became tiresomely triumphant, and just as objectionable as her brother, until a mouth full of takeaway cheese pie, followed by ice cream, prevented her talking.

They had all expected the Brake parents to be worried by their long absence and they were rather hurt when they found them quite unconcerned, taking a relaxed siesta on the terrace, shady now that the sun was in the west.

Mr Brake greeted them with a grunt and went back to sleep, Mrs Brake stirred herself enough to ask if they had had any lunch. She seemed dissatisfied with the cheese pies and said, 'You'd all better have boiled eggs with your teas. We've bought some more of those delicious honey cakes, and Daddy's going to take us out for a decent meal tonight.'

'We'll need some food for tomorrow,' Jeremy told her. 'We're going on an expedition into the mountains, starting at eight. Can we do some shopping tonight? I'm fed up with boiled eggs.'

'And we'll need bottles and bottles of water,' added Mandy. 'I nearly died of thirst today.'

4

Poor Nico, poor ponies

The four travelling alarm clocks called the English children obediently at seven. Kate and Mandy hadn't slept well in their little room in the roof; Mandy's sunburn had kept them both awake, but they pulled on jeans and shirts and staggered sleepily down the open stairs to the dimness of the shuttered sitting room where the boys slept. Fergus had lit the calor gas and put on a saucepan of eggs and the kettle. Kate began to lay, carrying mugs and plates out to the terrace table. They had missed the dawn, but the sun, round and red, still hung low over the sea and the eastern sky was silver-pink, fresh with the new day.

Fergus made the tea and persuaded Mandy to take mugs of it to her parents, Jeremy buttered bread for sandwiches, complaining that it was stale and like a brick and it was ridiculous that there were no sliced loaves on the Island. Kate opened the cans of tuna and sardines and cut lumps of cheese. They packed the food and the bottles of water into two rucksacks and a beach bag. They had made enough for six, because, as Kate said, they couldn't very well not share with Nico and Sophia, if they had come without food.

They were just finishing breakfast when Mr Brake appeared. Hitting his head on the low lintel of the back door for about the tenth time, he staggered on to the terrace swearing loudly.

Fergus hastily poured him a second mug of tea, Kate

offered him a slice of melon or bread and honey.

'Great Dad, you're actually up on time,' Jeremy seemed to want to irritate, 'now let's hope that useless car starts.' Mandy began her usual whine for money.

The car started, and Mr Brake dropped them outside Mr Perdika's gate at exactly eight o'clock. The boys shouldered the rucksacks, Kate found herself carrying the beach bag.

'I think Mum and Dad were quite glad to get rid of us for the day,' said Mandy putting on her red baseball cap as they walked along to the Pappas gate.

'Well I suppose they want a peaceful time and we want an exciting one,' suggested Kate. 'You didn't tell them about the fight, did you?'

'No, Jeremy thought they'd fuss. At the moment they think Nico and Sophia are looking after us. I hope Nico isn't going to spoil everything by being gloomy again. I'm sure he can find another pony to ride and Vrondi will have a much better life with the circus. Sophia says the farmers put all their ponies out on the mountains in the winter and most of them don't feed them even when it snows; she says they get terribly thin.'

'Yes, but though they have such a hard life they do seem very good-tempered and contented,' Kate pointed out as she opened the wire-netting gate and Mandy pushed back a couple of young goats.

Yani and Rozi were waiting in their stable, but there was no sign of Nico or Vrondi.

'Oh dear, I hope nothing awful has happened,' said Kate anxiously.

'Why should it; you're always imagining the worst, Kate. Do cheer up. Aren't you glad that you don't have to groom or tack clean here. You and Fergus always seem to be brushing or scrubbing away when we see you at Mrs Kark's.'

'We don't mind, you get to know the ponies much better if you help to look after them,' answered Kate giving Rozi a crust of bread.

Sophia, Jeremy and Fergus, all mounted, were waiting by the Perdika gate. One look at their serious faces told Kate that something *was* wrong. 'What's happened?' she asked.

'It is horrible,' Sophia's voice almost broke. 'Vrondi is sold, Mr Pappas has been offered more money, but, much worse, my grandfather has learned that the circus is not buying the ponies to perform, but to feed to the lions and tigers. They will be killed one by one and eaten by the beasts.'

Mandy gave a little shriek of horror. Kate sat in silence feeling sick.

'Mr Pappas has not yet told Nico of his decision. We learned all this from grandfather,' Sophia continued, 'so Nico is hiding and we are going to take Vrondi to the mountains and set him free. Andony will be coming soon, full of spite and triumph, to take Vrondi to his death, but he will not find him. We must hurry to the beach, Nico is waiting for us.' She set off along the road at a jog trot.

'Poor Nico, poor ponies,' said Kate almost in tears.

'We can't let it happen, we'll have to do something.' Fergus sounded determined.

'But what?' asked Kate.

'I don't know, I'm trying to think.'

'We'd better tell the police. If it's illegal to export mares they'll have to do something,' decided Jeremy.

'That won't help Vrondi.'

'No, but it'll save some of them.'

They rode between the houses, past a little hotel and down the ramp to the beach.

'Are you all safe?' asked Sophia. 'Safe to gallop?'

'Yes,' they answered. Kate and Fergus rammed on their straw hats, Jeremy took off his dark glasses. They looked along the beach; it was still early, there were few swimmers, no sunbathers. Sophia set off at a steady canter, choosing to ride on the hard sand, close to the sea, rather than on the soft powdery kind under the cliff. The rest of them followed, but Libertas, fighting Jeremy for his head, soon took the lead. Kima cantered neck and neck with Mya, Rozi scurried after them. Then, as Sophia increased the pace, Yani, whose solid body, with a leg at each corner, wasn't built for speed, began to be left behind.

Kate was delighted with Rozi, the little grey was much faster than she had expected and obviously thrilled to be galloping. Her stride was short but quite smooth and Kate, crouched forward, felt happily at one with her, as with outstretched neck, she raced after the Perdika ponies, her flying hoofs almost silent on the sand.

They left the town beach and came to a narrower stretch of sand, which seemed to be favoured by campers who had erected their tiny tents, in the shade of rocks and boulders, close beneath the cliffs. Sophia had slowed to a canter when Kate heard a splash and a wail behind. She looked back. Mandy was out in the shallows, picking herself up and trying to retrieve her baseball cap, which bobbed away on the water. Yani, further out, was raising a spectacular splash as she high-stepped through the waves. Kate pulled up and turned back.

'A beastly dog came out of that tent and made her shy,' wailed Mandy. 'I'm soaking, I sat in the sea.'

'Never mind, you'll soon dry in this heat,' shouted Kate turning Rozi into the waves and trying to head off the dun pony. But Yani was too pleased with her

59

freedom. She dodged, raced for the shore, and then with a couple of triumphant but ungraceful bucks, she charged past the Perdika ponies and disappeared round a rocky point.

'Oh why didn't you grab her?' wailed Mandy. 'Now she'll gallop for miles. Can I come up behind you, Kate? I can't walk all that way.'

'No, Rozi's too small and you're too heavy,' Kate shouted over her shoulder as she joined the pursuit. The other riders had already disappeared and she let the eager Rozi tear after them. Hurtling round the point, where there was only a narrow corridor of sand between the rocks and the sea, she almost collided with Nico. He was riding Vrondi and leading Yani. But Rozi swerved in to the water and then, recognizing her stable companions, came to an abrupt halt.

'Shall I take Yani back to Mandy?' Kate offered, stretching out a hand for the reins.

'No, the English no good, waste time,' said Nico in a savage voice. 'Libertas also.' He pointed over his shoulder, and, looking ahead to where the beach widened again, Kate saw a riderless Libertas being pursued by Sophia. Leaving Nico to sort out Mandy, Kate cantered on to help Sophia. On the way she overtook Jeremy who was trudging wearily through the soft sand.

'Mandy fell into the sea, she's got a wet bottom.'

'*I* didn't fall off,' Jeremy sounded indignant. 'There must have been a hole or something, he stumbled and fell on his nose; I hadn't a chance.'

'Kate, come and help me,' Fergus was shouting. Kate trotted across the fine, small-stoned shingle to the foot of the track which led up to the coast road on the cliffs above.

'I'm supposed to be barring the way to the road, but I

don't feel wide enough on my own,' Fergus told her. 'Kima's OK on the straight but she's almost impossible to manoeuvre. I don't think anyone's taught her the "lateral aids"; they need Mrs Kark out here.'

'Rozi's the same, she thinks the rider's legs always mean go faster, but I don't think Nico and co would listen to Mrs Kark, they don't think women can ride, much less teach riding. And now Nico's saying that the English are no good.'

'Well the Brakes *aren't* much good, bareback, and he's desperate to get Vrondi to the mountains; it is a matter of life and death.'

As Mandy and Nico reappeared round the point, riding soberly side by side, Libertas gave in and allowed Sophia to catch him. Jeremy vaulted on and then the whole party came across the shingle at a brisk trot, which had both the Brakes hanging on to their ponies' manes. Nico's face was so full of suppressed rage that Kate and Fergus let him pass without a word, and then jogged up the steep track after him in silence.

At last, when they were on the road, Fergus dared to ask the question that was in all their minds; he asked Sophia, 'Isn't Mr Pappas going to be furious?'

'Yes, but I think Nico has a story to tell him and there is a chance he will believe it so long as no one tells Nico officially that Vrondi has been sold.'

'Yes, I have a story,' Nico slowed up and let the other riders crowd round him. 'I am showing the English the spring at Nyphi and then the way into the mountains. Then Vrondi sees a mare, a new mare he does not know. He rear very high. I come off. He fight me, the rope break and he run away with the mare. Maybe I do a little work on the rope to make sure it break. But you all agree with my story, OK?'

The English children looked at his taut and anxious

face doubtfully. 'It won't be true,' Kate pointed out diffidently.

'You think I should not not tell lie to save Vrondi?' asked Nico in a passionate voice. 'Maybe you think I must let him be killed. It is OK for him to be eaten by the beasts.'

'No, I think we must save him *and* the other ponies,' answered Kate, 'but lies are so complicated, even ones that are meant to do good.'

'Yes, we'd better make it as near the truth as we can,' Jeremy supported Kate. 'Supposing we're questioned. We've all got to tell the same story.'

'If we could find a mare for him to go off with, it would be a help,' agreed Fergus. 'Then at least we'd all know what she looked like.'

'Let's act out the whole scene, then it will have happened in a way,' added Mandy.

'Yes that is a good idea,' said Sophia and explained their suggestions to Nico in rapid Greek. 'My grandfather has told me these things,' she went on in English, 'so he will not believe the story, but he will not give us away, because he disapproves very much of what is being done. The big problem will come if we meet a member of the Komas or Pappas families and Nico is told of the sale, or if Mr Pappas should come after us in his cousin's three-wheeled truck; these are the things that Nico fears.'

'But however good our story is it's going to look very suspicious,' Fergus pointed out, 'I mean Nico knew that Vrondi was very *likely* to be sold.'

'Yes, the whole thing stinks,' agreed Jeremy. 'Unless Pappas is a total idiot he's bound to smell a rat.' Sophia translated again and then Nico said, 'I think Mr Pappas will be very angry, I think I will lose my work; it will be very hard, but this I must do for Vrondi.'

Kate looked at the beautiful, black stallion, young and strong, walking proudly with his head high and his ears pricked and knew that it could not be right to kill him. He was so brave and full of life. They had to save him, they couldn't let him die. Then she began to think of the other ponies, the humble, patient, little mares like Rozi, that were also to be killed and a lump came into her throat and tears into her eyes. They *had* to be saved too, but she couldn't see how it could be done; she felt very helpless.

When the main road turned inland, to cross the narrow centre of the Island to the harbour, they took the rough, untarred road which led on along the cliff tops. On one side of them the dark-blue sea stretched away to the horizon, on the other side lay a tract of land, barren save for thorny scrub, spikey thistles and round pincushion bushes covered in lavender-blue flowers. And from the scrub came the noisy chorus of cicadas, almost drowning the sounds of lapping waves and scuffling hoofs.

As the day grew hotter the sight of sea and sandy beaches became more and more tempting.

'I'm dying for a swim,' Mandy muttered to Kate, 'but I expect Nico would kill me if I suggested it.

'I think he'd go on without you,' Kate told her, 'but I'm certain there are thousands of jellyfish down there too, so it's no *use* suggesting it.'

They came to a fertile area of land where a summer-dry stream bed was bright with pink and white oleanders and small, stone-walled farms had the usual stubble fields, olive trees, tethered goats and scratching chickens. All the time they were drawing closer to the mountains, which had lost the blue smoothness of distance and became harsh and craggy with great, grey rocks, and yellow-grey with scree sparsely covered with green scrub.

Three times, after leaving the main road, cars passed them and Nico took hasty refuge in the centre of the group of riders, leaning forward to reduce his height and hide his face. After the first time Mandy offered him her red baseball cap as a disguise and he took it quite gratefully to everyone's surprise.

Sophia called '*Kaliméra*' and made remarks which seemed to be about the weather whenever they passed one of the old ladies in black dresses, with black scarves tied over their heads, who seemed to be busily employed picking fruit, watering goats or sitting on their doorsteps gutting fish.

But it wasn't until a man appeared round a bend in the road, a straw-hatted farmer leading a mule loaded high with loose straw, that Nico showed any real fear. He looked round wildly from the high, brush-topped stone wall on one side of the road to the sheer drop to a rocky cove on the other.

'Is he a Komas, what shall we do?' asked Kate, horrified to see the hunted look on Nico's face. The others looked round and saw at once that there was no sideways way of escape.

'Shall I create a diversion?' suggested Jeremy and then, without waiting for an answer, he gave Libertas a violent kick. The surprised pony shot forward into a canter. Jeremy, clinging to the mane and shouting, 'Whoa, whoa!' looked quite a realistic runaway, but all the time his farside heel, the one the farmer couldn't see, was thudding against Libertas's side.

'I can't stop,' he shouted as the canter became a gallop. 'Whoa, whoa,' he repeated as he charged past the surprised-looking mule. The others took their cue from him, and shouting at each other in English, they raced in pursuit. The farmer shouted something as they passed, but none of them could have stopped his or her galloping pony even if they had wanted to. They sped on in a cloud of white dust until, round another bend, they found Jeremy dismounting and waiting.

Mandy arrived last, holding on to Yani's mane and giggling weakly. 'You should have seen their faces, I don't know who was the most astonished, the man or the mule.'

'Did you hear what he shouted?' Fergus asked Sophia.

'No,' she shook her head. 'But that was a good idea, Jeremy, it could have been quite a big problem if he had talked to us.'

'Yes, he got us out of a tight spot. Well done, Jem, quick-thinking.' Fergus was giggling as he patted Jeremy on the shoulder in a patronising manner.

'Oh shut up. Did you know the old man then?' Jeremy asked Nico as they rode on. It was Sophia who answered. 'He is a cousin of Mr Pappas and he has a telephone at his farm so it could be that he would try to stop us; to tell us that Vrondi was sold and we should return home.'

'We arrive. Nyphi.' Nico pointed at the mountain, sheer rock, rising like a fortress, which towered above them apparently blocking their way ahead.

'We haven't got to climb up there, have we?' asked Mandy looking up at it in horror.

'No, there is a track, a pass, which leads into the mountains. It is the only way, you will see in a moment,' Sophia told her.

Fergus was staring about him as though he had to drink it all in and memorize the scene forever. 'It's incredible,' he said, 'really grand.'

'Yes, it's great,' agreed Kate, but she couldn't enjoy

the beauty and the grandeur, she was too worried about Vrondi and the other ponies, mostly the other ponies now that Vrondi was so close to freedom.

The pass appeared suddenly, a narrow gap between a vertical rock face and the cliff edge dropping away some forty feet to the sea. As they rode through the opening, Sophia pointed to a heavy iron gate. 'When that is shut in the winter the ponies have to stay in the mountains, there is no other way out.'

The ponies had pricked their ears and begun to hurry.

'They are thinking of the drink they will have in a moment when we come to the spring,' Sophia explained as the sheer rock gave way to a jumble of broken rocks and boulders. The leading ponies turned off the road and hurried into the cool, dark rock cavern, jostling for first drink at the clear pool.

'Water OK,' said Nico greedily drinking handfuls of water taken from the bubbling spring itself.

'We could water our horses at the troughs on the other side of the road,' Sophia told Kate as they waited their turn, 'but they are for sheep, flocks of sheep, and the horses prefer the pool.'

When Mya and Rozi had drunk their fill, Kate and Sophia led them back to the track where they found Nico at work on his reins. He was sawing the rope backwards and forwards over a sharp-edged rock.

'I make sure it break,' he explained.

'There don't seem to be any mares about,' complained Mandy who was wearing her baseball cap again.

'There's a donkey up there,' Jeremy pointed to a high rocky ledge beyond the spring where a large donkey gazed out to sea, ears pricked and with a very contented expression on his face.

'He's admiring the view,' said Fergus.

'I expect a mare will come before too long,' Sophia told them. 'In the summer this is the only water in the mountains, the streams have all dried up, so all the animals must come here to drink. We will wait in the shade,' she added, leading the way across the track to a huge fig tree whose great, gnarled branches and broad, glossy leaves shut out the sun. Between the fig tree and the cliff was a small grassy plateau and on it was a square of stone thoughs all brimming with water which had been piped under the road from the spring.

'Perfect for sheep,' announced Fergus admiring the arrangement. Jeremy had led Libertas to the cliff edge and was looking over the sagging wire fence at the sea.

'Oh do come on, I'm dying of hunger, do bring the rucksacks,' wailed Mandy at the boys. 'It smells of goat in here,' she complained to Kate who led Rozi into the fig-tree cave.

'Never mind, there are plenty of seats for humans,' said Kate sitting down on one of the huge twisting roots. 'We've brought enough lunch for you and Nico,' she told Sophia.

'Good, I am very hungry too. I will take something to Nico. I think he wants to stay by the road and watch for a mare.'

The honey cakes had oozed on the lumps of goat cheese, but the riders were all so hungry that everything tasted delicious even the tough, stale bread. The ponies, pleased with the shade, hung their heads, half closed their eyes and fell asleep.

'They're much better behaved than English ponies,' observed Kate remembering a picnic ride when Sparrow had grabbed half her sandwiches and then, finding they were filled with ham, had spat them out all over the other picnickers.

'If only they were a bit bigger, I'd love to school Kima and teach her to jump,' said Fergus.

'Yes, and had saddles and bridles; I'm so stiff,' added Mandy stretching out her legs, 'I don't think I'll ever be able to walk again.'

'Oh stop moaning, it's no worse for you; we're all in the same boat,' Jeremy snapped at her.

When Kate had finished she went with Sophia to see how Nico was getting on. He was sitting on a rock in a small patch of shade and seemed quite contented, but Vrondi was becoming restless. He was looking up the track and giving loud hopeful neighs at regular intervals.

'He has no interest in our mares now they are in foal,' Sophia told Kate, 'he would be pleased to find a new one.'

'Why doesn't Nico just turn him loose?' asked Kate.

'He has to make sure Vrondi goes right into the mountains,' explained Sophia. 'If he stays down here and goes wandering round the farms looking for mares, he will soon be captured.'

'But supposing no mare comes?' asked Kate, 'they may all be in foal.'

'Sooner or later one will come,' answered Sophia confidently.

'I'm worried about the other ponies. We can't let them be killed. I think we ought to go and look for them, or find Petro and see if he he knows where they are.'

Sophia translated Kate's words for Nico and when he understood them his dark eyes flashed and his lean, brown face hardened.

'I save Vrondi,' he answered her fiercely. 'The others,' he made an empty gesture with his hands, 'they are not my friend.'

'I understand that you don't love them like you do

Vrondi,' Kate spoke slowly, 'but they are ponies; we love all ponies and we want to save them too.'

'He does care about them, once he is certain that Vrondi is safe he will help us find the others,' Sophia told her.

'But time is passing, I think *some* of us ought to go and look for Petro,' argued Kate.

'I agree,' Mandy, bored with the goat-smelling shade, appeared beside them.

'But I cannot go with you and stay with Nico,' protested Sophia. 'Wait a little longer, please.' She broke into Greek and then back into English, 'If you like we will ride a short way into the mountains. That way we may find a mare quicker.'

'Great!' Kate and Mandy ran to tell the boys who shouldered the limp rucksacks and vaulted on.

They rode up the dusty track and as they climbed higher the narrow pass opened out, the mountains stood back from the track, billowing one behind the other like huge waves. Plants, spiked and prickled, grew on their inhospitable slopes, and dark-green bushes, which had been clipped into strange stunted shapes by browsing animals.

The sun was overhead, it burned down on them and Mandy began to complain. 'I'm melting,' she wailed.

'We should have waited in the shade; it is always better to wait,' said Sophia. 'But look, both Vrondi and Libertas are sniffing the air, I think there must be horses near.'

Kate scanned the scrubby mountainside. Invisible sheep dogs barked, a flock of finches twittered as they feasted on thistle seeds, the cicadas whirled. The only sign of human life she could see was a double row of small green beehives, but there was no pony. They rode on in silence, trying to endure the heat stoically and listening to the scuffle of unshod hoof on the track.

Then at last they heard a neigh. The two stallions stopped dead and neighed loud and commanding replies before prancing on up the track with necks arched and tails carried high. The next neigh was nearer and, looking across to a clump of bushes, the riders could see swishing tails and then small heads with pricked ears watching them over the leaves.

The stallions neighed excitedly. 'You must hold on tight to Libertas,' Sophia told Jeremy. 'My grandfather would never forgive me if he escaped into the mountains.'

Nico had slid off and was exciting Vrondi, encouraging him to rear up and fight for his freedom, persuading him to tug at his rein. The rope refused to snap, so, picking up a stone, Nico sawed the rest of the way through. Free, Vrondi didn't gallop off in pursuit of the mares as they had expected, he stood undecided, looking from Nico and their ponies to the strangers halfway up the slope. Nico said something in Greek. 'We must wave our arms, shout, throw things at him,' Sophia explained. 'We have to drive him away. Not you Jeremy, you must hold tight to Libertas.'

They waved their arms, they shouted, but Vrondi didn't go. He stood looking uncertainly at Nico, waiting for his command. And the boy stood, tears running down his cheeks, unable to break the bond and drive the pony away. Then at last he made himself. In a voice full of anger and pain he shouted some Greek insult at the pony and taking the length of broken rope, swung it in the air and cracked it down across his quarters. Startled and hurt, Vrondi shot away up the slope at a canter. Then he stopped, turned and looked back at them. They waved their arms and shouted, somehow they had to convince him that he was no longer wanted.

But he stood watching them, disbelieving and puzzled, until one of the mountain mares whinnied softly. Then he turned and trotted to join them in their patch of shade.

The riders watched in sad silence. Nico was the first to turn away. Tying the length of rope carefully round his waist, he said, 'Now we find Petro,' and set off walking down the track towards Nyphi at a brisk pace. Sensing that he wished to be alone, the others followed him slowly. Kate kept looking back, fearing that Vrondi would change his mind and come galloping in pursuit. But, when they came to the pass and still no neighing, black figure had appeared, she stopped worrying. With Vrondi safe and happy with his new friends, they could concentrate on finding the other ponies.

They all drank at the spring and then rode out through the gateway back into the world of farmland and stone walls, topped with their untidy hats of brushwood, designed to keep mountaineering goats at bay.

Sophia told Nico that he was to ride Mya and she would walk for a time. At first Nico refused, he seemed to be saying he was too tall, but then he gave way.

'And when Sophia's tired I'll walk and you can have Yani,' Mandy told him.

'Yes, we'll all take turns,' agreed Fergus.

Nico made Mya lead and took a path which turned inland along a narrow valley. The day was growing hotter and hotter and they rode slowly. They swopped ponies, Nico riding each one in turn except for Rozi, who he said was too small and old to carry him. As Kate insisted on doing her share of walking, Fergus rode Rozi and Nico had two turns on Kima.

When they came in sight of the pine forest, they began to look out for Petro. At intervals Nico put two fingers in his mouth and gave an ear-splitting whistle, but there was no reply and though they listened intently they couldn't hear the bark of his dog or the baa of his sheep. It wasn't until they were below the forest that they heard an answering whistle and saw Petro standing in the arched entrance where Nico and Andony had fought. He waved and came skipping down a zig-zag path followed by a barking dog and a younger brother.

Except for Jeremy, whose turn it was to walk, they urged their ponies into a trot and up the hill. As soon as they met, the four Greeks began to talk excitedly. Petro kept pointing to the barren hill on the opposite side of the valley. Mandy, unable to bear the suspense, tugged at Sophia's T-shirt. 'What are they saying, do tell us?' she pleaded. But Sophia, who was listening carefully, ignored her. At last they drew breath and Sophia changed to English.

'Petro thinks the Komas's are keeping the horses in the deserted village,' she told them. 'You cannot see it from here, it is in a hollow over the brow of that hill. He has seen a truck carrying water go along the road and a mule loaded with straw has twice taken this path.'

'We must go and look,' said Kate forgetting the heat. The others looked doubtfully at the hill.

'We need another pony,' wailed Mandy. 'We *can't* take it in turns to climb up there.'

'Nico says we should go and he will stay here with Petro and Dino, for it is only a question of looking.'

'But if they *are* there can't we turn them loose?' asked Kate. 'Wouldn't they go to the mountains on their own?'

'Doubt it,' said Fergus, 'judging by Vrondi's behaviour they would try to follow us home.

'The Komas's would round them up again and

everyone would be very angry with us,' agreed Sophia, as, leading Libertas, she turned downhill. Jeremy was sitting on a stone, waiting for them in the valley and Mandy hurried ahead to tell him the news.

'I think we should go back to town and tell the police what's going on,' he said grumpily as Sophia handed him Libertas's reins. 'If exporting ponies is against the law, they should stop it.'

'Only the export of mares is unlawful,' Sophia reminded him. 'And I do not think the police would act if the complaint came from us. If Mr Anesti was on the Island it would be very different.'

'Well surely someone must know where he is, someone must have his address. And if we can't phone or send a telegram we'd better write a letter.'

'Does he speak English?' asked Fergus, handing Jeremy a bottle of water.

'Yes, his English is good, but I do not think he can come back if his mother is so ill.'

'He can phone the police here and tell them to do something,' snapped Jeremy.

'Well I suppose we'd better get some idea of how many ponies they have hidden up there,' said Fergus taking a swig of water and passing the bottle on to Kate. 'We'll need some facts if we're going to write a letter.'

They all drank and then feeling better, they vaulted on. Sophia led them across the floor of the valley and then the ponies tackled another zig-zag up the barren hill.

When you were close to it, it didn't look so barren, thought Kate. There were a lot of small, prickly plants and Fergus, who was riding in front of her, kept shouting 'Lizard' as they flipped away from the ponies hoofs and vanished under stones.

The deserted village remained invisible until they reached the crest of the hill, then they found themselves looking down into a hollow, three sides of which were dotted with small one-storied houses all in a state of decay.

'Why did everyone go?' asked Kate.

'Plague,' answered Fergus.

'No, the spring dried up and you cannot have a village without water,' Sophia explained.

'*Where* did everyone go?' asked Mandy.

'To the town. Except for the fishermen and the farmers most of the Island people like to live near the town. Either the town or the port.'

'I'm not surprised they left, it looks a bit of a dump and it can't have been much fun living here miles from anywhere,' decided Jeremy.

Kate didn't want to waste time talking, so she led the way at a canter, down the sandy slope into the hollow and straight to the nearest cottage. The windows were broken, the door had been taken away; there were no ponies inside. She rode to the next cottage and the next. They were all the same: one door, two rooms with earth floors and small windows.

'They pong a bit,' called Mandy.

'They're falling down, all the roofs leak,' said Fergus. The three of them seemed to have left Sophia and Jeremy behind.

As she rode from cottage to cottage and found no ponies, Kate began to think that Petro had made a mistake. The left-hand cottages were all empty, the centre cottages were empty too. It wasn't until they approached the lowest cottages on the western slope that Rozi neighed and was answered by a whole chorus of anxious whinnies.

Kate cantered to the first building and found a

broken-down door wired across the doorway and wooden slats nailed across the windows. She peered in and saw in the dim light, a huddle of ponies.

'Some of them are in here,' she called over her shoulder.

'We've got to go, Sophia says we've got to go,' Mandy called back.

Kate rode on to the next cottage. There were ponies in there too; she tried to count them. A breathless Fergus arrived at a canter.

'Come *on*, Kate. We've got to go.'

'Why?' asked Kate indignantly. 'Just when we've found the ponies.'

'Something's happened, Nico was signalling from the other hill, Sophia saw him.'

Reluctantly Kate abandoned her count and followed Fergus. Jeremy was shouting from the ridge; they gave the ponies their heads and galloped full tilt up the slope and halted abruptly by the other ponies.

'What's the matter, what's happened?' asked Kate. Sophia pointed. A small truck loaded with a large barrel was chugging its way along the main track from the forest. The track didn't take a short cut like the zig-zag path, but a longer more level route, round the head of the valley.

'I think we should go now, before we are noticed,' said Sophia.

The ponies decided they were going home and raced down the zig-zag path at a reckless speed. The English riders held on to their manes and hoped that their mounts knew what they were doing.

'Well it was worth it,' said Kate when they had rejoined Nico in the shade of the pines. 'We know the ponies are there and they're all on that side,' she pointed to the right. 'There were about six to eight in

75

the cottages I looked into, but it was rather dark and I
didn't have time to count properly.'

'Knowing they're there doesn't do much good,' complained Mandy. 'What are we going to do about them?'

Sophia looked at Nico, who shrugged his shoulders
helplessly.

'We need to know which day and what time the
ponies are going to be shipped,' said Fergus.

'And we need the address of the president of the
Horse Society,' added Jeremy.

Sophia repeated their words in Greek, and then said,
'I will ask my grandfather about the address and we
will both try to learn what plans have been made about
the boat to Athens. Now we go home.'

'Would you like a go on Yani, Nico?' offered Mandy.

He shook his head. 'Nico wishes to walk,' explained
Sophia. 'It is important that he should look very weary
when he tells his story to Mr Pappas.'

'Supposing he's there when we get back?' asked Kate
anxiously, 'he may ask us where Nico is.'

'You tell him the story in English and look very
worried as you do now. He will not understand a word,
but he will see that things have not gone too well,'
answered Sophia.

5

I need your help

The Brake parents, having had a restful day without their children, were in a very amiable mood when the exhausted riders returned. They made them tea and announced that, to shorten the queue, they had already showered. Then they listened to the news that the ponies were to be killed and fed to circus animals and to Mandy's sad account of the freeing of Vrondi. They agreed that Jeremy's plan to write to Mr Anesti was a sensible move. Then Fergus described the beauties of Nyphi to Mr Brake and Kate remembered to ask after Mrs Brake's foot, which was better: another three spikes had come out.

Later they drove into town for dinner and chose a restaurant where you could eat outside on a flat roof and watch the people in the narrow streets, crowded in the cool of the evening.

They had eaten their first course and Mandy was making a fuss because the fish she had ordered had come with its head attached. To keep the peace Fergus offered to exchange it for his stuffed tomatoes, but Mandy wanted Jeremy's chicken, which he was determined to keep. Bored by the Brake battle, Kate was looking round at the other diners, wondering what they were talking about, when she caught sight of Nico. He stood at the top of the steps looking from table to table as though searching for someone. She smiled and waved. A look of relief came over his face as he saw her, but it faded as he wound his way through the tables, and despondency took its place.

'My English is not good, so I bring you letter,' he said glancing at them in turn. 'Sophia write it for me,' he added, handing it to Fergus, and then stood silent, as though waiting for an answer. Jeremy said, 'This is Nico, Mum, you remember him at the races.'

'Yes, of course. Hullo, Nico.' She smiled at him.

Mandy had left her place and was leaning over Fergus's shoulder.

'I need your help,' she read aloud.

'Shush, it's *secret*. Don't yell it out,' Fergus objected.

'You stupid twit, trust you to give the whole thing away –' began Jeremy.

'For goodness sake don't start quarrelling now,' Kate snapped at him, 'can't you see that something awful has happened.'

Fergus passed the note across the table. Kate and Jeremy shared it. 'Dear English,' they read, 'I need your help. Mr. Pappas and his uncle are going to keep watch at the spring at Nyphi and catch Vrondi when he comes to drink. To prevent this I have to to carry water higher up the mountain at dawn and in the evening and keep guard at night. They say the boat will come this week and when it has gone Vrondi will be safe. Please help. Sophia will explain if you go to her grandfather's house at 4 p.m. tomorrow, ready to ride to Nyphi. Yours hopefully, Nico.'

'But how *can* we help? I don't understand, what does he want us to do?' asked Mandy.

'Shush, the waiters are probably Andony's cousins,' Fergus muttered at her.

'The letter says Sophia will explain,' Kate pointed out. 'All we have to do is to be there at four. Of course we'll help, Nico,' she told him.

'Yes, of course,' agreed Mandy.

'Perdika's at four, tomorrow,' said Fergus.

Jeremy, who was re-reading the letter, corrected him. 'Four English time, 1600 hours Greek time,' he insisted.

Nico nodded and then vanished down the steps.

'What's this all about, kids? That pony again?' asked Mr Brake.

'Shush, there are informers everywhere,' Fergus told him.

Jeremy leaned forward and spoke quietly, 'I don't suppose it's as bad as Nico and Sophia make out, but the Komas's do seem to run the Island. One of them is mayor and apparently no one will stand up to him but this Mr Anesti.'

'Small town politics,' said Mr Brake, 'well, it can happen.'

'It certainly can, a sort of Greek mafia. I hope you're not getting mixed up in anything dangerous.' Mrs Brake sounded worried.

'Oh don't be a twit, Mum, it's nothing like that,' said Jeremy through a mouthful of fried chicken.

'But if we've got to prevent Mr Pappas from catching Vrondi it could be –' began Mandy.

'You've got the wrong end of the stick as *usual*,' Jeremy spoke scornfully. 'Can't you read? He said "water".'

'Shush,' the others shouted at them. 'Shush.'

They composed the letter to Mr Anesti immediately after breakfast on Wednesday morning. It began by being long and rambling, but after the third re-write it became short and to the point. And, when it had been copied out tidily by Jeremy – they decided he had the best handwriting – they were all pleased with it and felt it was quite impressive.

Mr Brake, agitated over an invasion of ants apparently immune to his beetle spray, decided that he must go into town at once, so they all went with him and posted the letter in time to catch the lunchtime boat to the mainland.

After a few hours with Jeremy and Mandy squabbling about nothing and moaning that they couldn't swim, the Brake parents were only too glad to deposit the four riders outside the Perdika gate at four o'clock. Sophia was waiting for them in the garden.

'Nico stayed at Nyphi all through the night,' she told them. 'His mother thinks he was keeping watch with the two Mr Pappas. She thinks he's trying to *catch* Vrondi. Mr Stephen Pappas is the uncle of Nico's boss. He is an old man but unfortunately still good with the lasso. They expect to catch Vrondi easily, with no trouble at all, Nico says, especially as he is wearing a headcollar.'

'Can you explain about the watering?' asked Jeremy.

'Well, you understand there is no other water on the mountains, the ponies must drink at the spring and usually they come down early in the morning and in the evening. Nico has taken up buckets. Yesterday he filled them by torchlight. Petro's older brother took him up to Nyphi on the back of his motorbike so he got there before Mr Pappas. Then Nico stayed awake all night and at dawn, when Vrondi came, he caught him, gave him water and kept him with him while the two mares went down to drink. Today it is very difficult. The old Mr Pappas has stayed there and Nico could not refill the buckets. Also he has to do some work on the farm. I cannot refill the buckets because if I am seen there will be many questions.'

'But we can, we're just dotty tourists,' suggested Fergus.

'Exactly. You say "camping" they all understand camping.'

'Where are these buckets?' asked Jeremy suspiciously.

'They are behind a rock, a large rock on the right hand side of the path about half a kilometre from the spring. Nico has marked it with chalk, VN.'

'Half a kilometre,' groaned Jeremy, 'that's .3107 of a mile.'

'You cannot be nearer, the men would hear you.'

'We'll manage. Come on Mandy, let's get our ponies,' said Kate.

'But how long do we stay there?' asked Fergus.

'Until Nico comes. He will be there about seven,' answered Sophia. 'He will again spend the night there.'

'Mandy, it's your turn to carry the rucksack,' shouted Jeremy, but his sister hurried down the road pretending that she hadn't heard.

It was strange to be heading for the beach on their own without Sophia or Nico to act as a guide. Kate wondered whether they really knew the way to Nyphi. If you were following someone, you didn't notice all the crossroads and side turnings. She tried to visualize the way they had ridden the day before. Had it really been as straight and uncomplicated as she remembered? It would be terrible if they lost themselves and arrived late, to find that Vrondi had been recaptured.

There were a few sunbathers on the beach, but no swimmers; the pink multitude of jellyfish still swayed threateningly along the water's edge.

'Ugh, aren't they revolting.'

'Beastly things, spoiling our holiday.'

'But for them we wouldn't have made friends with Nico and Sophia, we wouldn't be riding to Nyphi now.'

Kate couldn't enjoy loitering on the beach. 'We must keep going,' she said. 'Supposing Vrondi comes down to drink early. Do come on.'

Let's have a race then,' suggested Jeremy. 'That'll get us moving.

'I'll give you all a start: fifteen lengths for Rozi and Kima, twenty-five for Yani – her maximum speed is about ten miles an hour.'

'I don't care if she's slow, she's super otherwise and I love her,' said Mandy, throwing her arms round Yani's neck.

'Where's the finish?' asked Fergus, forcing down the crown of his straw hat.

'The place where the beach narrows, where the rocks stick out into the sea.'

'OK.'

They raced. Rozi went her fastest scurrying gallop and Libertas only managed to overtake her in the last few yards, but Kate still wasn't enjoying herself. She kept thinking of Vrondi and of the other ponies shut in the dark, dirty cottages with only straw to eat.

On the road she ignored Mandy's moans about her stiff legs and insisted on trotting some of the way, but her worry about getting lost disappeared, for with the mountains ahead and the sea beside them, there was really no problem.

When they came in sight of the towering, fortress-like crags of Nyphi they all began to worry.

'I do hope we can find those buckets.'

'Where do you think the ancient Pappas is lurking?'

'He's probably sloped off to the nearest taverna.'

They entered the narrow funnel of the pass cautiously, fighting with the thirsty ponies who could see no reason for delay, but the circle of rocks round the spring was deserted and the ponies jostled each other

82

out of the way as they hurried to the pool, and thrust their noses deep in the cool water. The riders drank too.

Libertas had drunk first so Jeremy was first back on the track. When the others joined him, emerging reluctantly from the damp cool of the rocks into the sun, he held up a hand. 'Shush, listen.'

They listened and heard a loud rhythmic snoring noise ending in a whistle. 'It's him,' whispered Jeremy, 'look under the fig tree.' They peered into the dark cavern, roofed by branch and leaf, and saw a figure lying on a pile of striped blankets. Small, swarthy and unshaven, wearing baggy trousers and a grey shirt, it had to be the ancient Mr Pappas; an empty retzina bottle lay beside him.

'He's having a long siesta,' Mandy giggled.

'Great, let's hope he keeps it up and we can get the water without him seeing.' Glad of unshod hoofs they stole away and then rode up the track all looking for a rock marked with VN.

'Wouldn't it be awful if the chalk marks had worn off,' worried Kate.

'Must you?' asked Mandy. 'You're always so gloomy Kate.'

'She can't help it, it's her nature,' Fergus stood up for her. 'Look there it is.' He threw himself off Kima, flung her reins to Kate and scrambled up the outcrop of rocks. He vanished for a moment and then re-emerged carrying a stack of plastic buckets.

'Six,' he said, counting them out into pairs. 'Three of us go for water and one holds the ponies.'

'I'll stay with the ponies,' offered Mandy quickly. 'But will you all untie your reins so that I can let them graze; if there's anything to graze *on*.'

'Rozi loves those yellow thistle flowers,' said Kate

handing over her rope and picking up a couple of buckets.

'Camping,' Jeremy reminded them as they wandered downhill. 'If there are questions, we all look stupid and answer "camping".'

'Poor Nico, it must have been lonely sitting up there all night,' observed Kate. 'I wonder how he kept awake with no one to talk to.'

'Sophia said he had a torch so perhaps he read,' suggested Fergus.

'Or walked up and down to keep awake. I'm glad it's not me; he's got several nights to go yet,' observed Jeremy.

Old Mr Pappas was still snoring , so they filled their buckets in silence, topping them up from other buckets until they were all brimming, and then started back.

'That's great,' said Fergus as soon as it seemed safe to speak. 'Now if the ponies do come down early we can refill for Nico without arousing suspicion.'

'It's opening time,' announced Jeremy as they stopped to rest their aching arms. 'Look, here are the first customers.' A tinkling bell heralded the arrival of five goats, grey white and piebald, who came strolling down the track.

They looked hopefully at the buckets with their strange, amber-yellow eyes, but when Kate said, 'Sorry, it's not for you,' they seemed to understand the tone of her voice and strolled on.

When they had hidden the buckets behind a rock Jeremy unzipped the rucksack and began to share out food. The ponies were hungry too; now that the sinking sun was moving westward and the mountains were casting long shadows, they decided that grazing time had come, and instead of waiting patiently, with hanging heads and half-closed eyes, they dragged their riders towards edible bushes and browsed busily.

'What *would* the Pony Club Manual say if it knew they ate all these poisonous-looking plants,' Kate called to Fergus, who had been dragged to a distant bush.

'Someone should write a holiday section,' Fergus shouted back. '"Greek ponies do not eat hay, pony nuts or grass, but exist on straw, thistles and thorny scrub".'

'"They do not wear shoes",' Mandy added.

'"Or tack",' Jeremy joined in.

'"Which makes the tack cleaning section of this manual superfluous!" thank goodness!'

'"They are rarely groomed, so no books on how to do it are necessary and you can throw this one away",' Jeremy added with relief, leaving Kate rather shocked.

The ponies, browsing steadily, dragged their riders in different directions until they were too far apart to talk. They watched for the appearance of Vrondi in a silence broken only by cicadas and the champ of jaws. Then baas and barks announced the arrival of Petro bringing his flock down to drink. The sheep skipped down the thread-like paths, converged on the track and needed no shepherd with crook and dog to turn them towards the spring. Petro saw the English party, he waved and shouted something in Greek. They waved back.

'I wish I knew some Greek,' said Jeremy dragging a reluctant Libertas over to share Rozi's chosen bush. 'I shall start learning it before I come again.'

'You mean to come back then?' asked Kate surprised.

'Wouldn't mind. I'd like to see some of the other islands too, provided they're not all besieged by jellyfish.'

The evening was growing cool and the shadows of the

mountains were spreading over the sea, when Libertas threw up his head, sniffed the air, and gave a challenging neigh. The other ponies whinnied too.

Their riders vaulted on and, riding back to the track, arranged a barricade of ponies across its narrowest point. Fergus placed the buckets in a tempting row along the rock side. There were more neighs, the scuffle of unshod hoofs and Vrondi, followed by two mares, appeared round a bend in the track.

There was an affectionate reunion, with whinnying and nose-sniffing, between Vrondi, Rozi and Yani, but Libertas , who felt he was now the stallion in charge of the party, stamped a forefoot and squealed with jealousy. The mares found the buckets and drank greedily. Vrondi went over to inspect, he sniffed the water scornfully and, deciding to go on to the spring, tried to charge through the barricade of ponies. They stopped him quite easily. Mandy grabbed the frayed length of rope which dangled from his headcollar and shrieking at Kate to take Yani, led him across to the buckets.

'Come on now, drink,' commanded Mandy. 'Don't be difficult, I know it's warm, but if you insist on fresh spring water you'll find yourself feeding tigers in Athens.'

Vrondi took a sip and pulled back. 'Oh, don't be obstinate,' Mandy told him, her voice growing irritable.

'Here, let me try,' said Fergus and, picking up another bucket, he offered it to Vrondi with soothing whoas. Vrondi laid back his ears and rolled his eyes – a day of freedom in the mountains had given him a taste for his own way. Suddenly he reared up, twisted, jerking the rope out of Mandy's hand, and swerved away. He whinnied to his mares; dutifully they left the water and followed him, as he circled at a high-cadence trot, snorting and jumping the boulders and bushes which blocked his path. Mandy dodged about making grabs at him, Fergus stood holding out a piece of bread he had intended for Kima, but the black stallion ignored them both; he continued to prance and snort and circle, showing off to the other ponies, who stood with ears pricked and eyes wide with admiration.

'What about leaving him for a minute and letting him calm down,' suggested Kate.

'But supposing we can't catch him, supposing he goes down to the spring,' wailed Mandy. 'I couldn't help letting him go, the headcollar rope was too short.'

'Why not catch the mares? He won't want to leave them and go on his own,' proposed Jeremy. But the mares were excited, rolling their eyes and tossing their manes. They refused to be touched. Left alone, Vrondi stood on a hillock, snorting, daring the humans to come and catch him.

If only we could *explain*, thought Kate desperately. All four riders were feeling desperate. Nico had trusted his pony to them, now they were failing him; if Vrondi was shipped to Athens and killed it would be their fault.

'With these rocks on either side and our ponies blocking the way the track makes a sort of corral. Supposing Mandy and I try to drive him into it and you two grab him,' suggested Fergus.

'You'll only make him more excited,' said Kate gloomily.

'Well what do you suggest then?'

'We could just wait and see what he does next. And eventually Nico will come.'

'I don't think he's going to give in,' said Jeremy

looking at the defiant pony who watched them from his hillock.

'Is there any water left in the bottle?' asked Mandy. 'I'm dying of thirst.' They passed round water and food.

Vrondi's mares had joined him and, suddenly, he left his hillock and set off purposefully. He led them higher up the mountain and then took a sheep path which wandered through a craggy barrier of rocks. He planned to outflank them, thought Kate, to join the track lower down, but *could* ponies climb rocks? Then she remembered the donkey on the ledge and, vaulting on Rozi, she walked a little way down the track watching for the ponies to emerge on the other side of the rock barrier. She waved to the other riders to come on, she didn't want to shout for that might alert the watching men at the spring. She could see the ponies again, they were picking their way through scrub and boulders towards Petro's path. It would bring them straight down to the track. Kate rode on. Vrondi reached the path, turned down it and began trotting. His head high, he watched Kate's every move; he was ready for confrontation. She took up position where the path joined the track. She would turn him, force him back up the track away from the spring. Then Vrondi began to canter, he looked very determined and Kate realized that he wasn't going to stop for waving arms. If she met him head on, it would be the smaller Rozi who was knocked over. He was coming faster and faster, thundering down the sheep path towards her.

You couldn't stop a runaway horse head on, she reminded herself. You had to gallop alongside him. But Vrondi was faster than Rozi. She turned back to the track and began to canter in the direction of the spring, looking over her shoulder to see what Vrondi was doing. He was coming fast, he skidded on to the track, then she could hear the sound of his hoofs, his rapid breathing behind her. He was gaining ground with every stride, she steered Rozi to the right, making room for Vrondi to pass on her left and with the rope reins in her right, held her left hand ready for a grab.

The black head was level with Rozi's quarters, it reached her flank, her shoulder. Kate leaned over and took the frayed headcollar rope and hung on grimly, gripping with her knees to prevent Vrondi's faster pace dragging her from Rozi's back. She kept the little grey going at full speed as she tried to slow Vrondi down, pulling on the short rope with all her strength, but with very little effect. 'Whoa,' she called, 'whoa,' horrified by the headlong gallop that was carrying her straight in to the Pappas's trap. At any moment the two men would hear the sound of hoofs and come running out to make an easy capture. Desperately, she tugged again, then she tried jerking at the rope. She slowed a little, but not enough. They were perilously near to Nyphi and Rozi was tiring.

Then Kate heard a third set of hoofs, more gasping breath, and on the other side of Vrondi, Libertas's bay head appeared. Then Jeremy, riding with all the energy he possessed, came alongside. He leaned over, grabbed the black pony's headcollar and began to pull. It made all the difference. Together they slowed him to a canter, then to a trot. They were so near the rock circle which guarded the spring that they hardly dared to speak. 'Round to the right?' asked Jeremy in a low voice.

'OK.' They wheeled the three ponies round, making a tight turn on the track, and fled from the dangers of the spring.

Mandy and Fergus came to meet them, moving the two mares from the track, they let the threesome canter all the way back to the bucket rock. There they dismounted and, after looking back down the track for pursuers, leaned against their blowing ponies.

'That was a near thing.'

'Terrifying.'

'I could see the Pappas's triumphant faces as I galloped up to the spring leading him,' said Kate. It wasn't quite true; she hadn't had time to think, only to act, but she could see them now. 'You are a stupid pony, Vrondi,' she told him. 'But Rozi was brilliant, a real heroine,' she added stroking the little grey's neck.

'It's a good thing Libertas is so fast. None of the other ponies could have overtaken Vrondi,' said Jeremy patting the bay proudly. 'When I saw you couldn't stop I really galloped, and having a bridle was a help too.'

'You gave us the most terrible fright.' Fergus had collapsed on a rock and was fanning himself with his straw hat.

'It was terrific when you caught him,' Mandy told Kate. 'For a minute I thought everything was OK and then realized you were being runaway with.'

'And it was Jem to the rescue,' teased Fergus.

'Can you hold Vrondi for a sec?' Kate asked him. 'I want to untie Rozi's reins and put them on his head-collar; we mustn't lose him again.'

When Vrondi was safely attached to a long rope, Fergus said, 'He'll have to have a special minder, two hold the ponies, two fetch water. Come on, Mandy, you and I had better go while the others recover.' Having poured the remaining water into two buckets and put it in front of the rather sulky Vrondi, Mandy and Fergus set off for the spring.

They had been away for about ten minutes when a head appeared above the cliff on the other side of the track and looked round furtively. Then, catching sight of the group of ponies, a look of relief spread over the face and the rest of Nico scrambled up on to the track.

'Hullo,' he said hurrying over to pat Vrondi. 'You catch him.' He seemed rather surprised.

'We had to.' Kate began to explain what had happened, but though she spoke slowly, Nico didn't seem to understand.

'You're wasting your time,' Jeremy told her. 'He doesn't understand a word and if he did he'd have a fit.'

'But supposing Vrondi tries it again?' asked Kate.

'He hung on to him last night didn't he? Look, he's got a long cord round his waist. Nico,' he went on, 'you take Vrondi, I fetch water, OK?'

Kate offered the water that Vrondi had left to the other ponies, passing the buckets round until the last drops had been sucked up and then handed the empties over to Jeremy. When he was out of earshot, she made another attempt to tell Nico how Vrondi had behaved, but he didn't seem able to make the effort to understand. He gave helpless gestures and then went on tying his cord to Vrondi's headcollar. When he had restored Rozi's reins, Kate let her four ponies graze, but they would pull in different directions, refusing to co-operate at all, and she began to wish that she was carrying water.

Mandy and Fergus returned, groaning about their aching arms.

'They're both there, playing backgammon and eating their suppers,' Mandy told Kate.

'They tried to question us, but we looked dim and repeated "Camping" like parrots,' added Fergus. 'Oh good, Nico's arrived. How did he get here?'

'Up the cliff, there must be a way along the shore.'

'You go now, very quick , night come,' Nico pointed at the sky.

'OK , as soon as we've got Jeremy,' Fergus agreed. 'He's coming now.'

Mandy vaulted on. 'We're going to be terribly late. Mum will be in one of her states, and I'm so tired,' she complained.

'You don't look half so tired as Nico,' Kate told her. 'Have you noticed the great black circles under his eyes?'

'He looks dead on his feet,' agreed Fergus.

As soon as Jeremy had deposited his water buckets, they said goodnight to Nico and waving, started for home. They didn't like the idea of riding past the spring.

'Supposing they rush out and stop us, we have been behaving a bit suspiciously,' asked Mandy, 'I think we'd better creep by in silence.'

'That's the worse thing to do,' snapped Jeremy.

'We don't want to be lassoed,' added Kate.

'I think we should ride fast and all talking, as though we hadn't a care in the world,' said Fergus.

And this was what they did, though Kate found it difficult to sound carefree and Fergus ran out of things to say and rode through the pass reciting rhubarb, rhubarb, and battling with Kima who decided that she'd like to stop for a drink at the spring.

The journey back to town seemed shorter than the outward one, for the evening was cool and the ponies in a hurry for suppers and stables. Sophia was waiting at the Perdika gate. 'Did it go well?' she asked anxiously. 'Everything was all right and you saw Nico?'

'Yes, mission accomplished,' Fergus answered.

'It nearly wasn't, Vrondi was awful. We couldn't

explain to Nico, but he nearly got away –' Mandy began to explain.

'OK, OK, don't make such a drama of it,' Jeremy interrupted her. 'Have you heard anything from our parents?' he asked Sophia.

'Yes, they have been twice to look for you. They seemed worried, but I told them that all was well and you would be a back before long. They will be here again in ten minutes,' she added looking at her watch, 'they have gone for a drink in the square.'

'We'd better hurry then,' Kate told Mandy and let the impatient Rozi jog on towards the Pappas's farm.

'We ought to have asked about tomorrow,' said Mandy catching up with her. 'Do you think we've got to do the same thing all over again?'

'Yes, until the boat's come and gone if we want to save Vrondi. But Mr Anesti should get our letter tomorrow. I do hope he does something. I want to save the other ponies too.'

6

That won't save the ponies

When Sophia came to the cottage on Thursday morning and, leading Mya down the steep garden, appeared on the terrace, the English children were still having breakfast. They had slept late and the Brake parents had become impatient and gone to town without them, though promising to return soon with provisions and news of the jellyfish.

They looked at Sophia in surprise and then, realizing from her red and swollen eyes, that she had been crying and something must be wrong, they all jumped to their feet and began to be helpful.

Jeremy poured her a glass of orange juice, Fergus took Mya and tied her to a post where she could browse on a patch of yellow-flowered thistles, Kate fetched another chair and sat her down at the table. Mandy put an arm round her shoulders and asked, 'What's the matter, what's happened?'

Sophia took a gulp of orange juice, looked round at their anxious faces, and said, 'The Pappas men have captured Vrondi. Poor Nico fell asleep. He had tied Vrondi's rope to a large stone so that he could graze. He meant to watch him carefully all through the night, but he fell asleep and when he woke at dawn Vrondi had gone. He is already handed over to Andony and we hear that now they have the twenty-five ponies, they have telephoned for the boat and it will come this very evening.'

'Oh Lord. . . .'

'How awful.'

'What are we going to do now?'

'Poor old Nico.'

'Yes, poor Nico,' repeated Sophia. 'He is in despair. He says Vrondi will die in this terrible way and it is all his fault for sleeping. I blame myself too. If only I had gone to help him. My father forbade me to go; girls on the Island do not do such things. If only I had disobeyed.'

'We'll just have to rescue them all,' said Kate.

'Brilliant,' Jeremy's voice was full of sarcasm. 'How? Are we going to have a pitched battle with the Island farmers?'

'We can't just go up there and take Vrondi back, that would be stealing,' Mandy objected.

'You mean you don't want to do anything. You're just going to sit there and let them be fed to circus animals?' demanded Kate.

'No, of course not.' Mandy sounded offended.

'The law *is* partly on our side,' Fergus's voice was calm. 'That is if you're sure that it's illegal to export mares.' He looked at Sophia.

'Yes, I am certain, but it does not help Vrondi,' she answered.

'It's a useful loophole,' observed Fergus.

'You mean that while we're trying to stop the illegal export of mares it would be too bad if we let out a few stallions by mistake?' asked Jeremy.

'Exactly, Kate says it's very dark in the cottages.'

'But when I suggested letting them out before you all said it was pointless,' Kate protested. 'You said the farmers would round them up again.'

'It's a question of timing,' Jeremy told her. 'If we drive them to the mountains while the boat's actually here, the captain's *bound* to get tired of waiting before the farmers can round them up.'

'And at least that'll give Mr Anesti a chance to reply.'

'If he can be bothered.'

'Oh yes, he will be very much bothered, I am certain of that,' Sophia told Jeremy, 'but as his mother is so ill it may be difficult.'

'What does Nico think we should do?' asked Mandy.

'He is in despair. He threatens to kill himself.'

'That won't save the ponies.'

'Stupid twit. The important things to know are what time the boat is coming and how they're going to get the ponies to the boat. If Andony's going to lead them there in relays, he'll be taking the first batch any minute now. And even if they're using a cattle truck it'll take several journeys.'

'Could you or Nico find out?' Kate asked Sophia.

'I will try.' Sophia wiped her eyes with a small handkerchief and got to her feet. 'I will go home and see Nico, he is hiding in our stable. I do not know what will happen to us if we let the twenty-five ponies go free.'

'We'll let them out,' Kate told her. 'No one can do much to us, because we shall soon be going home.'

'I can see that it could be difficult for you and Nico,' Fergus agreed thoughtfully. 'For one thing the farmers may have already spent the money Boukaris paid them and, if they haven't, they certainly won't want to pay it back.'

'But if the farmers have handed the ponies over to Andony, surely *he's* responsible,' suggested Jeremy.

'That really would be great,' said Fergus grinning cheerfully.

'Do you think it could be so?' asked Sophia looking a little less despondent.

'Oh I do hope it is. That really would pay him back

for what he's done to Nico.' Mandy began to dance about the terrace in delight.

'Great!' said Kate. 'But we haven't freed the ponies yet and time's passing; hadn't we better start walking to the stables?'

Mandy groaned, 'Oh we *can't* walk, my legs are so stiff I can hardly move,' she protested collapsing into a chair.

Fergus began to laugh, 'A minute ago you were dancing.'

Jeremy looked at his watch. 'They'll soon be back with the shopping,' he said, 'and then Dad can drive us over.'

'We could change and then start finding food and packing the rucksacks,' suggested Mandy, who had seen a look of obstinacy spreading over Kate's face. 'Then we'll be ready to start the moment Mum and Dad get home.'

'It's no use starting too soon, we've got to give Nico a chance to find out loading times,' Jeremy reminded them.

'But we know it's this evening and that's not far away,' said Kate, who wanted action. 'All right, Mandy, let's put on our jeans and make some lunch and then, if your parents haven't turned up, we can start walking. Are you sure your father will want to turn straight round and drive back?'

'He won't *want* to, but don't worry, we'll make him,' answered Mandy, 'it's much too hot to walk.'

Mr Brake was not as amenable as Mandy had hoped. He came down the garden path triumphantly waving the new ballcock he had bought for the faulty lavatory cistern and was followed into the cottage by his nagging children.

'I'll take you to the stables when I've fixed it and not

before,' Kate heard him shout as he banged the shower room door.

'We'd better walk,' she said.

'Oh he won't be long,' said Mandy optimistically. 'Dad, how long will it take to fix it?' she called through the door. There was no answer. 'I'm sure it won't take long,' she assured Kate and joined Jeremy in inspecting the shopping which Fergus had carried down from the car. 'Any honey cakes?' she asked, 'I'm dying of hunger.'

The long silence from the shower room was suddenly broken by a burst of furious cursing. Then Mr Brake emerged waving two ballcocks aggressively. 'That moron in the ironmongers has sold me the wrong size; it's useless, won't even fit in the cistern. I'll have to go straight back and change it.'

'Terrific! We're coming with you,' shrieked Mandy.

'You're such a twit, Dad, why didn't you take the old one with you the first time,' Jeremy reproached him.

Sophia seemed more cheerful. 'Still no word from Mr Anesti,' she told them. 'But I have given all the ponies a big feed, the Pappas ponies too, and Nico has gone to make enquiries. I expect him back any moment; your plan has given him hope.'

When Nico returned he was running. He looked hot and exhausted and talked to Sophia in rapid Greek.

'The boat is expected at Ormos Gilfada soon after four o'clock,' she translated. 'The truck is small and must make many journeys. We should start at once and go through the pine forest; that is the shortest route.'

'Where's this Ormos Gilfada?' asked Jeremy.

'It is a small deep-water harbour on the west of the Island – the opposite side from Nyphi. But as the Island is narrow at that point it is not far from the deserted village. In the old days the harbour was used for ships taking stone to the mainland, but now it is not used. There are no customs men or port officials; no one to object to the export of mares.'

'These Komases are crafty,' said Fergus.

'Come on, Mandy, let's get our ponies,' called Kate. She was already running up the road, the rucksack bumping about on her back.

'No rush, no one will do a thing until after the siesta,' answered Mandy following slowly.

'How's Nico going to get there?' Kate asked Sophia when, mounted, they met again in the road.

'He says he will run: he knows a short cut to the forest and it is better if he is not seen with us. He will be there when we need him.'

They set off on the road round the town, Libertas and Mya jogging as they vied for the lead. They took the track past the cemetery, crossed the main road and plunged gratefully into the shade of the pine forest, a gratitude which abated as they found themselves assaulted by hungry mosquitoes and surrounded by hordes of buzzing flies.

They climbed and climbed, reached the plateau and came to the spot where Nico and Andony had fought.

'Let's have lunch here; it's getting late and I'm dying of thirst and hunger.'

'There's no water for the ponies here,' Kate pointed out.

'No, the nearest water is at Nyphi and we have no time to go there, they will manage until evening,' Sophia told her.

'We've got to eat somewhere, if we don't we'll become inefficient.' For once Jeremy supported his sister.

'And this is the last bit of shade,' added Fergus, looking across the sunscorched valley to the barren hill opposite.

Dismounting they handed round food and water bottles. The ponies, glad of a rest, hung their heads, half closed their eyes and dozed. The riders, tense and anxious, ate quickly all wondering what lay ahead. Could they really free the ponies or would the Komases be there on guard? What would happen if the truck arrived and they were caught in the act?

Kate didn't feel hungry, in fact she felt slightly sick, but agreeing with Jeremy that the unfed become weak and inefficient, she forced down a sardine sandwich and a hard-boiled egg.

'Where will the truck come from?' she asked Sophia trying to get the whole scene straight in her mind.

'I am not certain. If it comes from the town or from the Komas farm it will come up this track through the forest and then round the head of the valley like the water truck we saw. If it comes from Ormos Gilfada there is a track from the sea which joins this one at the head of the valley; they both cross the dry stream bed by the stone bridge. Look.' She led Kate to the edge of the trees and pointed away to the right. 'Where those walls are, that is the bridge.'

'When everyone had finished eating, they mounted and rode on, down the zig-zag path into the valley. There was no sign of Petro or Dino, but they could hear the sleepy baa of grazing sheep and the occasional bark of a dog.

They crossed the valley and, as the ponies tackled the hill with their usual courage, Kate found she was feeling more and more apprehensive. She felt sure things were going to go wrong. In between looking over her shoulder for an approaching truck, she wondered what they would do if Andony was there on his own. Could Fergus and Jeremy hold him down, while she and Mandy and Sophia freed the ponies?

It was a long climb but the ponies didn't suggest stopping for a rest until they reached the ridge and then the riders were able to look down into the hollow that hid the village.

'Still deserted,' said Fergus in a relieved voice.

'No Komases and no truck,' agreed Kate. Suddenly she felt excited. 'Are we going to let them all out first and then round them up and drive them to Nyphi in one great bunch?'

'Yes,' the others agreed.

'I think one person must hold the horses and stay on guard,' said Sophia. 'From here it is possible to watch the road and give good warning of the truck's coming.'

'I'll stay,' offered Mandy.

'You know where you've got to look?' asked Jeremy as they all dismounted.

'Of course,' Mandy answered haughtily.

'We'd better not undo the reins in case we have to make a hasty exit,' said Fergus, taking his over Kima's head.

'It's very silent.' Kate took another look at the village lying quiet and deserted in the baking heat. 'I hope they haven't taken them already; I hope we're not too late.'

The others looked at her in horror, but at that moment, Libertas, who had been sniffing the air, suddenly neighed. On the right, from cottage after cottage came choruses of answering neighs. Anxious and hungry neighs, thought Kate and shouting, 'It's all right, we're coming,' she ran down the sandy slope.

Fergus caught up with her as she reached the first cottage, Sophia and Jeremy went on to the next.

'Look at that.' A stout plank had been nailed across from door post to door post. 'They've used six-inch nails,' groaned Fergus. 'We need a crowbar to shift that.'

Kate was struggling with a hingeless, latchless door. 'I'm moving this,' she said, 'but it's going to fall inwards on the ponies.'

'Doesn't matter, it's quite light and pretty rotten,' observed Fergus as it splintered beneath his hefty kick. They dragged the broken bits of door out of the way and both tugged at the plank without shifting it at all. The smell of dirty stable filled the air and the ponies waited anxiously in the dark and stench; they seemed to have no food or water.

'We're never going to get them out in time,' Kate stopped tugging at the plank to lick a long nail scratch on her arm. Fergus had ducked under the plank and was in the cottrage trying to kick it outwards.

'I think we could get them underneath it, none of them is very tall,' said Kate, looking at the huddled group of blinking ponies. Squelching across the sodden floor, she grabbed the smallest pony by her forelock and dragged her towards the door. 'Come on, your withers will go under, you've got to lower your head,' Kate told the bemused pony. Fergus got behind her and pushed. Kate found a piece of bread in the pocket of her jeans and held it low. The hungry pony followed it eagerly, out into the bright light and freedom.

'Hurrah!' Fergus brought another pony to the bar and Kate, who had only rewarded the first with a measly crumb, held her piece of bread low and per-suaded the second pony to lower its head and squeeze under the plank. Fergus was slapping and shouting, trying to encourage the others to follow. Suddenly one, bolder than the rest charged, flung herself under the plank and, neighing loudly, cantered across the hollow. This inspired the others and one by one they bent their knees, ducked under the plank and escaped.

'That's six,' said Fergus counting.

'They look awful, so dirty and thin: that beastly Andony,' stormed Kate as they ran to the next cottage.

'Jeremy and Sophia haven't got theirs out yet. Our ponies came *under* the plank,' Fergus shouted to them.

'This plank's lower,' said Kate as she began to unwire the door which still had hinges.

'Perhaps they'll jump it. As soon as the wire was untwisted Fergus forced the door open and climbed in among the ponies. This lot, conscious that some of their friends were free, tried to barge their way out almost crushing him.

'We've found a sledgehammer,' Jeremy was shouting in triumph, as another six ponies streamed out into the hollow.

'Either get out of the way or jump it,' Fergus was shouting at his ponies. Excited by the scene outside one of them tried to jump. Rearing up she got her forelegs over and then, finding herself straddling the plank, panicked, scuffling and kicking until she collapsed in a heap, her weight causing the plank to splinter and give way at one end. With Kate pulling at her forelock and Fergus slapping her rump, they got her to her feet and out of the doorway allowing the other five ponies to come crashing out of their prison.

'Is Vrondi in your lot?' Sophia's voice sounded anxious.

'No, we've let out twelve. How many did you have?'

'Twelve too.'

'They've put him somewhere else.'

Or taken him straight to the boat, thought Kate. Andony, determined to prevent any attempt at rescue by Nico, was capable of that.

They ran from cottage to cottage looking for another prison. Sophia was calling 'Vrondi' in her Greek voice.

Suddenly there was an answer, a whinny came from a cottage in the top row.

'Oh hell, not right up there.'

'Some of us had better start to round up the others.'

'You must put Libertas in the lead, they are more likely to follow a stallion.'

'OK,' Jeremy handed the sledgehammer to Fergus. 'We'll get moving and hope you catch us up.'

'What will you do with our ponies?' asked Fergus, shouldering the sledgehammer and following Sophia up the hill.

'Tie them up,' shouted Kate running towards Mandy. 'Tie them to the plank the ponies crawled under.'

'Thank goodness you've come at last,' said Mandy as they vaulted on their ponies, 'Libertas has been awful.'

Kate explained about Vrondi and about leaving Kima and Mya tied up. They dragged them down to the first cottage and tied them to the plank with lengths of wire to allow for a quick getaway. Then, shouting and waving arms, they tried to drive the aimlessly milling ponies to the left-hand side of the hollow where a path led along the ridge towards Nyphi.

Libertas, wildly excited at the sight of his huge herd, was prancing and bucking. He didn't want to lead the way and an exasperated Jeremy slid off and began to drag him in the right direction. Mandy had dropped her reins on Yani's neck and was waving both arms like a windmill. 'Go on you stupid ponies, don't you want to be saved? Go on, follow the leader.'

It was Kate, turning back to pick up a long stick lying on the ground, who saw the truck. It was turning slowly out of the forest. It didn't look like an English cattle truck, but it was larger than most of the vehicles on the Island and had a green canvas awning. The steady banging of the sledgehammer told her that Fergus was still trying to free Vrondi.

'The truck's coming,' she shouted, 'the truck's coming.'

Jeremy vaulted back on Libertas and when he jibbed again gave him a very determined whack with the end of the reins. The pony shot forward and then, accepting defeat, walked briskly along the path. The other ponies seemed to be calming down, regaining their sense of direction. One or two, pricking their ears and thinking of water set off after Libertas in a purposeful manner, Kate brandished her stick at the laggards, turning them, hurrying them on. Then she looked back, the truck was making its way steadily towards the head of the valley; it would reach the village in a matter of minutes. She could see figures still hammering at the cottage. She turned again to the freed ponies. The last of them were on the path now, the first had caught up with Libertas. They jogged in a long line, thinking of the spring and hurrying to quench their thirst. Kate caught up with Mandy and handed her the stick.

'They look all right now, I'll go back and help the others.' Without waiting for an answer she turned Rozi and galloped full tilt into the hollow, past Kima and Mya and up the other side. Fergus was climbing into the cottage through a window.

'The truck is almost at the bridge,' she told him.

'Too bad,' he said taking the sledgehammer from Sophia and vanishing.

'They've put two planks across this one and nailed up the door itself.' Sophia's voice was full of despair. 'We can't open it from the outside.'

The sledgehammer began to crash against the panels of the door. They bulged and split, but there wasn't going to be time to get Vrondi out, thought Kate.

Perhaps, if there was no hope, Sophia and Fergus ought to go, they oughtn't to be caught here, redhanded, breaking down the door. But if they left Vrondi to his fate, Nico would never forgive them. She rode up to the ridge and looked over. The truck had reached the bridge, but at the same moment as it entered the narrowing road between stone parapets there was a great chorus of baas and from the other side came Petro, crook in hand, leading his flock of sheep, while behind, two little brothers and the dog kept the animals in a tight bunch. They came to a halt on the bridge and using the parapets as a sheep pen, began a complicated operation of grabbing sheep, or was it the rams, by their hindlegs, shouting excitedly, letting them go and then wading into the flock to grab another. The baaing, shouting and barking grew louder and louder, then the driver of the truck began to hoot his horn impatiently, but Petro and his assistants continued to grab legs; they behaved as though the truck didn't exist.

Kate rode back to the cottage. 'Petro's holding up the truck with his sheep, he's blocked the bridge, you've got a few minutes more. I'll fetch your ponies so we can make a quick getaway.'

Fergus didn't stop hammering, but Sophia said, 'It is moving a little.' Kate rode down to fetch the ponies, and as she did so, a running figure appeared over the ridge. For a moment she thought it was Andony, come to drive them away and stop the rescue, but then she saw it was Nico panting, grim-faced and with a head-collar slung over his shoulder.

'Vrondi,' she shouted pointing. And, as he sprinted on, Sophia called to him in Greek.

Kate's heart rose. He was taller and stronger than any of them; surely he could smash down the planks. She untied the two ponies and hurried them up the slope. As she reached the cottage there was a crack, the sound of splintering wood and a cry of joy. Nico appeared in the doorway, bending back the shattered planks, behind him, Fergus was buckling on Vrondi's headcollar.

Throwing the sledgehammer to one side, Nico took Vrondi and vaulted on. Sophia and Fergus ran to their ponies. Pausing for a moment on the ridge, Nico gave his piercing whistle, and then they were galloping, all four of them, as fast as they could go. Down into the hollow, up the other side and then in single file along the path to Nyphi. They rode recklessly along the twisting path with its outcrops of rock, the ponies' hoofs kicking up a cloud of white dust, and they didn't slacken speed, until, seeing a bigger cloud of dust ahead, they knew they had caught up with the other ponies.

'Did you get him?' Mandy's voice came out of the cloud.

'Jeremy, they've got Vrondi and Nico's here too,' she shouted up the line. 'Oh isn't it great, I never thought we'd do it.'

'We haven't yet,' said Fergus looking behind him, 'they drive on such ghastly tracks here I wouldn't be surprised if they tried to follow us.'

'Nico says there were four men, not three, and Andony in the truck,' Sophia told them. 'He does not think they will pursue us on this track for it grows rougher, but he thinks they might try to cut us off when we come down to the pass. He wants to go faster.'

Nico had begun to ride Vrondi through the other ponies he made his way to the front and then, sharing the lead with Jeremy, he increased the pace.

To their right rose the first of the mountain ranges, sheer rock and impassable, to their left the dried up valley and now, ahead, they could see the sea and the towering crags that guarded the pass at Nyphi. They were cantering downhill, a great swell of ponies, not racing or jostling, but moving as one body, sharing the scrape and scuffle of hoofs on the rocky path, the pant and wheeze of their breathing, the thick steam and the smell of the stable which rose from them.

Kate left everything to Rozi. She felt she could trust the little pony completely, and kept watch for a truck speeding to cut them off, or a band of angry farmers gathering to demand their ponies.

She looked at the track along the cliffs, at the small, white farm houses, down in to the valley. The whole countryside seemed to have been scorched into stagnation, it was still and empty everywhere, except in their small private world, caught in the turbulence of the cantering ponies.

At last their path joined the coastal track. And, enveloped in another cloud of white dust, they slowed to a trot and passed into the shadow of the crags. Nico and Jeremy swung round the fig tree and led the cavalcade to the stone troughs. Some of the ponies broke away and jostling their way into the circle of rocks, fought to drink at the spring itself, but most followed the ponies with riders, rushed to the troughs and drank greedily.

They drank and drank. Then they stood, water trickling from their lips, gazing at the mountains and the sea with a new pleasure and awareness. Then they drank again.

Kate watched them. Black, brown, bay, grey and dun, there was still a trusting look in their brown eyes as they swished their tails and flicked their manes contentedly. They had no idea of what had been planned for them. They would have trusted Andony, following him on to the boat, incapable of suspecting his and Mr

Boukaris's horrible intentions. Now they were simply grateful for their release from dark and smelly prisons. She felt like crying as she looked at them. Their manure-stained coats were sweaty and coated with dust, shortage of food had run up their stomachs and pinched in their flanks. How could people do this to them? Arrange such a horrible and uncomfortable journey with death at the end of it?

Nico, who was stroking Vrondi lovingly – the black pony was still shining and handsome, his captivity had been too short to leave a mark on him – spoke to Sophia in Greek.

'We must drive them to safety now,' she translated.

'But if the farmers want to catch them again won't they just come at dawn?' asked Mandy. 'We can't water *this lot* with buckets.'

'But by then the boat will have got fed up and gone, we hope,' Fergus pointed out. 'Boats usually have other cargoes lined up, people waiting for deliveries. They can't hang about waiting for farmers to catch ponies.

'We have gained time, that is all,' said Sophia.

'And now we'd better think of how to use it,' agreed Jeremy.

'I wonder what they said when they got there and found all the ponies missing; I expect they got in the most terrible rages. I thought you had all been caught and dragged off to prison and Jeremy and I would have to deal with twenty-four ponies,' Mandy rattled on as Nico led Vrondi back to the track. 'Why were you such ages?'

'They had really barricaded him in, I think they guessed that Nico might attempt a rescue. If Jeremy hadn't found the sledgehammer we'd never have freed him.' Kate answered. 'Where did you put my brandishing stick?' she asked looking round, 'I think we're going to need it to get this lot going again.'

'Nico says we are to find some old tin cans with stones in them. They are hidden by the spring,' called Sophia. 'The men use them to frighten the ponies into the mountains at the end of the summer. He also says you are to wave your stick and shout, the more we frighten the ponies the better; if they are too trustful they will very soon be caught.'

'Here, give me that stick, I'll get them going,' said Jeremy taking it from Kate. 'You do some yelling Mandy, you've got a loud voice.'

Kate went with Sophia to look for the tin cans. Some of the ponies were following Vrondi up the track. Fergus was shooing on the ones who had stopped to browse on the bushes near the spring, the Brakes, with fierce cries and threatening gestures, were driving on the stragglers from the troughs.

Soon they became one cavalcade, jogging up into the cooler evening air of the mountains.

At the bucket rock Nico stopped and unbuckled Vrondi's headcollar.

'Now we must be careful and hold tight to our ponies, especially Libertas,' said Sophia looking round at the other riders.

Nico was waving the rope reins at Vrondi, trying to persuade him to go. The black stallion turned and stood scanning the mountain slopes, then he neighed and back came two faint answers. The rescued ponies pricked their ears and began to look more purposeful. Groups started to form of ponies which already knew each other. An elderly grey-muzzled stallion moved off with a couple of mares.

Nico looked apprehensively towards Nyphi and said something to Sophia. 'We must rattle our tins. Nico is afraid that the farmers, hearing what has happened, may come to reclaim their horses,' Sophia told Kate. They handed their ponies to Fergus and Mandy and moving up the track began to rattle the stones. It wasn't a particularly frightening noise, thought Kate, but the ponies seemed to recognize it as a signal. Suddenly they were all trotting and cantering. They spread out as they took their separate paths, and for a time the whole mountainside seemed to be dotted with flowing tails, but then, gradually, they disappeared, lost to view amongst the broken ground, the green scrub, the rocks and crannies.

Mandy heaved a huge sigh of relief, 'Thank goodness for that.'

'Well, they're safe for a few hours,' said Kate taking Rozi.

'Oh don't be dreary, Kate. It must be longer than that. Are we going home now, Sophia?'

'Yes, we go home home now to face the music,' agreed Sophia.

'But what about Nico, he's ponyless again?' asked Fergus.

'Nico says he is happy to walk, he is going to see Petro to thank him and to find out if the boat has sailed. If it has gone he will walk back to town and, if things are difficult, he will sleep in our stable. If the boat waits he will sleep here and try to keep all the ponies in the mountains at dawn. But he does not think the boat will have waited.'

'He's got more stamina than I have,' said Fergus admiringly. 'I'm whacked even though Kima's done all the real work. I'd be dead if I had to walk home now.'

'It's the excitement wearing off, your adrenalin is slowing down, you're not really tired,' Jeremy told him firmly.

'I wish mine would start up again then,' said Mandy with a yawn.

They parted at Nyphi. 'Goodbye for now, maybe I see you later,' said Nico and with a wave, he took the path up the valley towards the pine forest. The others started along the coast road, sitting loosely on their ponies, almost too weary to speak.

'What are we going to do if Mr Pappas has heard we're responsible and is furious?' asked Kate anxiously. 'We've got to put the ponies away.'

'Chuck the reins at him and run,' advised Fergus. 'One angry farmer's not too difficult, it's if they all come at once and try to lynch us, that frightens me. If we have to leave the Island in a hurry are your parents going to be very put out, Jem?'

Jeremy shrugged his shoulders, 'There had better be a letter from Mr Anesti when we get home,' he said. 'I'll feel like killing him if he lets us down.'

7

Let's take him home

Kate and Mandy crept into Mr Pappas's yard in a state of terror. Pushing their way through goats and a friendly donkey, they watered the ponies, then fed them and did their best to rub down their sweaty coats with handfuls of straw.

Kate hugged and patted Rozi sadly, wishing that she had a pocket of tit-bits to give her. She had been so good, so willing and obliging; but it seemed unlikely that Mr Pappas would hire them ponies any more, and Kate felt very mean at not being able to reward her.

They crept out of the yard, looking anxiously over their shoulders, expecting Mr Pappas to rush out of his house raging at them in Greek. Then, safely through the wire-netting gate, they ran up the road giggling with relief and found the Brake parents sitting outside the Perdika gate in their car.

'How did you know to come and fetch us now?' demanded Mandy as the boys appeared from Sophia's stable.

'Whew, you kids seem to have stirred up a proper hornets' nest,' said Mr Brake ignoring his daughter's question.

'Are the farmers furious, do you think they'll lynch us?' asked Fergus nervously.

'No, your Mr Anesti won't let them, he's a real charmer,' answered Mrs Brake. 'He looks like one of those tall, proud Spaniards you read about in books; I didn't know there were Greeks who looked like –'

'Mum, do you mean you've seen Mr Anesti, that he's actually here?' Jeremy shouted his mother down.

'Yes, darling. He came out to the cottage, full of apologies for disturbing us.'

'He arrived on the lunchtime boat and went straight to see the mayor and the chief of police.' Mr Brake took over the story. 'They tried to tell him he was too late, that the ponies had already gone, but he said he'd telephone the minister of agriculture in Athens, apparently they're on good terms, and have the boat sent back, as the mares on board had no export licences.

That called their bluff and they sent off a cop on a motorbike to whatever the place is called to hold the boat.'

'Ormos Gilfada,' said Jeremy.

'But the ponies weren't there. The chaps who'd gone to fetch them in a truck swore they had disappeared. Anesti thought this was just another attempt by the Komas lot to lead him up the garden path. He gave them hell until your friend Sophia's grandfather, who had somehow got in on the scene, suggested that you kids might have taken the law into your own hands. And the two old boys bumped all the way over to whatever the place is called to make sure the boat went back empty.'

'Ormos Gilfada. Our letter worked then,' said Jeremy proudly.

'It would have been too late on its own though,' Kate pointed out, 'we did need to free the ponies too.'

'Did Mr Anesti say anything about stallions?' asked Fergus.

'Not that I remember. Why?'

'It means Vrondi's still in danger.'

'But if the boat's gone it's not going to come back just for Vrondi, is it? It wouldn't be worth their while,' decided Mandy. 'Let's go home, I'm dying of hunger.'

'Hop in all of you,' said Mr Brake. 'Now Mr Anesti's here you can leave it all to him. After all he is president of the Horse Society and he's evidently quite a big noise on the Island.'

'Big noises look after big numbers, they don't always bother about individuals,' argued Fergus.

Exhausted, they all slept late and were still in bed when Mr Anesti appeared on Friday morning. Mrs Brake shrieked the news of his arrival up the loft stairs and Kate and Mandy, pulling on shorts and T-shirts, rushed down to meet him. The boys, who had put on shoes as well, followed them.

Mrs Brake had sat Mr Anesti down in the best of the terrace chairs and Mr Brake had poured him the last of the duty-free whisky. But he got to his feet at once and shook all their hands in turn, beginning with Mandy. He was elegantly dressed in pale-lilac shirt and a silver-grey suit, but he had taken off his jacket, and a panama hat. 'I am on my way back to Athens,' he explained, 'but I thought I would like to meet my correspondents and tell them that everything was now under control. This morning I had a telephone conversation with the minister of agriculture and I think I have convinced him that our horses are unique, part of our national heritage, and cannot be allowed to die out. This is the only island which possesses such a breed and there is nothing like them on the mainland. The experts at the Museum of Archaeology in Athens believe them to be direct descendants of the horses of Ancient Greece. "Absolutely unique," I told him, "and you are letting them be used as animal feed." He agreed to tighten up the regulations, especially at the mainland ports.'

'What about the legal position?' asked Fergus, 'I mean do the farmers have to pay back the money?'

Mr Anesti laughed, 'The Komas family is not too pleased with the position. Some of the farmers are buying their horses back, others have refused and cannot be forced to do so.'

'What about Mr Pappas?' asked Kate. 'Is he buying his black stallion Vrondi?'

'I am afraid we have a problem there. Mr Pappas does not want the horse and Mr Komas is inclined to keep him for his son if he cannot find a purchaser.'

'Oh no!'

'Andony owning Vrondi, Nico would never get over it.'

'Dad, if he's for sale why can't we buy him,' demanded Mandy. 'Ponies here aren't nearly as expensive as in England and he's terrible fast, he'd make a super Prince Philip Games pony. Oh Dad, do buy him. It would be great prancing round Ralston on a black stallion.'

'We've nowhere to keep a pony, much less a stallion, and how much do you think it would cost to get him home?'

'We could stable him, he could have half the garage,' wailed Mandy.

'Dad has said no, Mandy, and he means it.' Mrs Brake was trying to sound firm.

'I'm not sure that Vrondi would like Ralston, it's very different from the Island,' Fergus pointed out, 'and he might be a bit frustrated with no wives. Then there's the weather.'

'Young Nico Maragos would like to buy the horse, he tells me has money saved, but it is not enough. And he cannot ask his family for help because his father and two uncles were all drowned many years ago in storm at sea. Mr Perdika thinks well of the boy and says he is willing to help with a loan and so I think I must also take a share. Young Nico has some scheme for making money and says he will pay us back, but of course we cannot be sure of this and we take a risk.'

'Well if it's not too hefty a sum, I'd be glad to contribute,' said Mr Brake suddenly. 'Nico seems to be a worker and he and Sophia have given our kids a great time here. Yes, if you'd like me to chip in, I will.'

'Oh Dad, you are sweet. What a brilliant idea,' shrieked Mandy throwing herself upon him. 'Oh you are terrific and won't Nico be *pleased*.'

'He's very proud, he may not like taking money,' said Fergus.

'A loan would be OK, surely,' argued Jeremy.

'Leave it to Mr Anesti,' commanded Mrs Brake and for once she was listened to.

Mr Anesti, who had been making calculations, passed his notebook to Mr Brake. 'It is drachmas,' he said, 'and I think it is a very reasonable sum. A little more than the horse dealer paid, but Mr Perdika, who is a wise man, feels that Pappas should buy the horse back from Komas and then we will pay the price for a riding horse which is slightly higher than for meat. This way there will be no bad relations between him and young Maragos.'

'Good idea, I go along with that,' agreed Mr Brake.

'Excellent. Well I now go to see young Maragos and his boss and then I catch the boat. If you would see Mr Perdika, he will be handling the financial details for the syndicate.' He got up and bowed to Mrs Brake. 'It has been a great pleasure to meet you and your charming family. I am most grateful to the young people for alerting me to this breach of the Island's law and wicked plot to rob us of a unique heritage.' He shook hands all round and then Mr Brake escorted him to his car.

'Posh,' said Fergus when he was out of earshot. 'Very classy indeed.'

'A bit pompous, I thought,' observed Jeremy.

'Oh darling, how can you? It's old-world courtesy. I wish there was more of it around,' protested Mrs Brake.

'I thought he ought to have been a bit *more* grateful,' complained Mandy. 'He made it sound as though we just wrote a letter and he did the rest. Not a word about all those miles we rode, water buckets we carried and ponies we freed.'

'He did say he was *most* grateful,' Kate pointed out.

'And perhaps he wants to forget the illegal things we did,' suggested Fergus. 'After all they've got to go on living together when we've gone home.'

'Let's have breakfast. Any eggs, Mum?' asked Jeremy. 'Oh good, peaches, and this awful stale bread.'

They had finished breakfast and were discussing whether their legs were strong enough to stroll down to the beach and see if the jellyfish had gone, when they heard a voice, calling their names in turn, from the road above. Kate ran to look and then, shouting, 'It's Sophia and Nico,' dashed up the hill to the gate. The others raced after her.

'Mr Anesti has been to see you? He has told you everything?' asked Sophia.

'I'm not sure about *everything*, he told us about the minister of agriculture and the export licences,' answered Jeremy.

'And about buying Vrondi,' added Kate.

'And Dad decided to join the syndicate. It was great. He doesn't usually do things out of the blue like that and, perhaps if he has a share in Vrondi he'll want to come back to the Island,' exulted Mandy.

'Are you pleased Nico?' asked Fergus stroking the stallion's black neck.

'I am very happy,' Nico answered carefully. 'And Mr Pappas is also happy. I work for him. Vrondi lives with Sophia. We are . . .' Running out of words, he turned to Sophia. 'You tell.'

'Nico and I are going to breed ponies, but we are also going to run a trekking stable. We will take the children of the tourists trekking round the Island. It will be a proper business. It is you who gave us the idea, you enjoyed it all so much. My grandfather approves and we can hire many extra ponies in the summer. Nico is going to learn more English and I will improve my French and learn a little German, so it will be possible to take children of all nationalities.'

'It sounds a terrific idea,' said Fergus enthusiastically.

'Especially when the jellyfish come,' added Mandy.

'And it'll give the ponies work. The farmers won't grudge them their food so much if they earn money, will they?' asked Kate.

'I think you ought to invest in a few saddles and bridles,' said Jeremy. 'People from abroad will expect them.'

'We will think of that, but first we must pay off our debt,' answered Sophia. 'Now tomorrow we want to show you the other half of the Island. We will take you for a long trek starting at eight, is this OK?'

'Yes, of course.'

'We'd love to come.'

'That'll be really nice,' they answered.

'We'll see you then,' Sophia waved as she turned Mya.

'Goodbye until then,' called Nico and Kate saw that he was actually smiling. 'I hope we can afford all this riding,' she said, suddenly worried.

'Yes, don't worry. Dad says it's miles cheaper than in Ralston and as Sophia's lending her ponies we're going to give her a really nice prsesent when we leave.'

'What about a bridle?' suggested Fergus.

'*And* we're going to have her to stay with us,' announced Jeremy, 'and take her riding at Mrs Kark's.'

Mandy was counting on her fingers. 'There are only four days more,' she moaned suddenly. 'We started on a Thursday so we have to leave on a Wednesday. Only four *days* left of the best holiday I've ever had.'

On the following pages you will find details of other exciting books from Sparrow.

THE NO-GOOD PONY

Josephine Pullein-Thompson

It was never going to work. The Brodie children disliked the
Dalton children at first sight. The Daltons were smooth and
elegant, their ponies well schooled and their tack immaculate.
The Brodies always looked a mess, their tack was falling apart
and they did not even have a pony each.

But now that Mr Dalton had married Mrs Brodie, the
children were all going to live together. The holidays would
be ruined, and even riding would not be fun any longer with
the Daltons about . . .

THE PRIZE PONY

Josephine Pullein-Thompson

Debbie read her letter again, to make sure she'd made no mistake. 'Mum,' she said at last. 'Mum, read this. I *think* it says I've won first prize. I *think* I've won a pony!'

Winning the story competition seemed like a dream come true for Debbie. At last she would have the one thing she had always wanted: a pony of her very own.

But once she got her new pony home, Debbie realized that she had more than she had bargained for. An inexperienced rider, she was no match for the excitable and spirited five-year-old. Before long Debbie is convinced that the pony is nothing but a disaster. Instead of the lovely rides she had imagined, she seems to spend all her time either falling off Easter, or chasing him up and down muddy lanes. Debbie is just at her wits' end when her mother has an idea . . .

A FOAL FOR CANDY

Diana Pullein-Thompson

'I reckon that cream mare is in foal.'

Fred's words rang in my ears as I walked down the lane. I dreamt of the beautiful foal that my favourite pony Candy would produce. Then a terrible thought crossed my mind. Perhaps we could not afford to keep a pony and foal through the winter months. It was more important than ever that my brother David and I should help to make the Pony Seekers agency a success . . .

A Foal for Candy is the second book about Lynne, David and Briony Fletcher – The Pony Seekers.

THE PONY SEEKERS

Diana Pullein-Thompson

Lynne and David Fletcher saw a terrible summer looming
ahead, a summer in which there would be no riding because
their parents could no longer afford to keep ponies for them.
But the day is saved when their elder sister, the famous ex-show
jumper, Briony Fletcher, decides to enlist their help to set up
The Pony Seekers, an agency to supply clients with ponies
ideally suited to their needs.

All goes well with the first few ponies, but then things begin
to go wrong, and Lynne and David realize they must do
something desperate if Briony's enterprise is not to be doomed
to failure . . .

Diana Pullein-Thompson is one of the three famous Pullein-
Thompson sisters who are among the most successful writers
of pony stories in Britain.

THE TEAM

K. M. Peyton

Ruth Hollis has grown too large for her much-loved pony, Fly-by-Night, and needs to find a replacement. At the Marshfield auction Ruth sees a pony she thinks she recognizes. It has a resigned and beaten look now, but she can sense the spirit and strength still there beneath the surface. Impulsively, she buys the pony – and then must face up to what she's done.

Buying the new pony means that Ruth must part with Fly, and then go on to discover whether or not the new chestnut is really the pony for her. As Ruth and her new pony try to become a team, the Area Trials become a testing point for both of them.

A PATTERN OF ROSES

K. M. Peyton

'T.R.I. 17 February 1910' were the words written under one of the drawings in the Ingrams new family home, *Inskips*. They were also the initials that fifteen-year-old Tim Ingram found engraved on a mossy tombstone in the local churchyard. The tombstone revealed that T.R.I. had died one month short of his sixteenth birthday. Tim found himself strangely drawn to this mysterious boy who had lived in the same house and had had the same initials as himself. Why had he died so young?

Assisted by his friend Rebecca, Tim set out to find out more about T.R.I. — and found himself involved in an astonishing and dangerous mystery.

'A magnificent new novel' *Daily Telegraph*

The Sparrow Bookshop

Sparrow has a whole nestful of exciting books that are available in bookshops or that you can order by post through the Sparrow Bookshop. Just complete the form below and enclose the money due and the books will be sent to you at home.

THE SECRET OF LOST LAKE	Carolyn Keene	95p ☐
THE WINKING RUBY MYSTERY	Carolyn Keene	£1.00 ☐
THE GHOST IN THE GALLERY	Carolyn Keene	£1.00 ☐
STAR TREK SHORT STORIES	William Rotsler	£1.00 ☐
A PONY FOUND	D. Pullein-Thompson	95p ☐
SAVE THE PONIES	J. Pullein-Thompson	£1.00 ☐
A NIGHT ON THUNDER ROCK	Enid Blyton	95p ☐
DRACULA	Bram Stoker	95p ☐

Humour

FUNNIEST JOKE BOOK	Jim Eldridge	£1.00 ☐
BROWNIE JOKE BOOK	Compiled by Brownies	95p ☐
SCHOOL FOR LAUGHS	Peter Eldin	95p ☐
NOT TO BE TAKEN SERIOUSLY	Colin West	£1.00 ☐

And if you would like to hear more about our forthcoming books, write to the address below for the Sparrow News.

SPARROW BOOKS, BOOKSERVICE BY POST, PO BOX 29, DOUGLAS, ISLE OF MAN, BRITISH ISLES.

Please enclose a cheque or postal order made out to Arrow Books Limited for the amount due including 8p per book for postage and packing for orders within the UK and 10p for overseas orders.

Please print clearly

NAME ....

ADDRESS ....

....

Whilst every effort is made to keep prices down and popular books in print, Arrow Books cannot guarantee that prices will be the same as those advertised here or that the books will be available.